The Girl Who Chased Away Sorrow

The Diary of Sarah Nita, a Navajo Girl

BY ANN TURNER

Scholastic Inc. New York

Grandmother weaves her story

I am home now from the white man's school, sitting beside Grandmother in the shade near our hogan. Slowly, skillfully, she spins wool, winding the long thread on a stick by her leg. Her legs are so thin, they worry me. For Shimasani *is old; soon her bones will be buried in the land of our ancestors.*

"My granddaughter, this summer I want to tell you all that happened during the Long Walk so you can write it down in the book that white teacher gave to you. You know some things, but not all. How the soldiers burned our crops and drove away our animals, making us starve. When they came looking for us, we had no choice but to go with them."

"To Fort Sumner," I add. Her eyes are half closed, remembering.

She reminds me that our people called the fort Hwéeldi, *a place of suffering in the Starving Time. Grandmother tells me she can remember the journey because she gave names to everything that happened: the Day of Burning, for when the soldiers came, and Silver Coat Finds Water, for when her dog found a stream.*

"I will tell it to you so you will be there with me. I will weave the story into you, like a spun thread, to make you strong, for when we remember, we are strong."

Grandmother's story begins in the Time of the Parting of the Seasons. I write down that the month is what white men call October, and the year is 1864. The leaves on the aspens are yellow, and she knows something evil is coming; she can feel it on her skin like a cold wind.

"Begin with these words, my granddaughter. 'My mother bends over the plants on the mesa.'"

My pencil flies over the page as I write down everything Shimasani says. I only hope that this book is big enough for all the things she will tell me.

Sarah Nita's granddaughter

New Mexico
1864

Mother tells me about Spider Woman

My mother bends over the plants near the red mesa. The sun is bright, and her shadow long. I remember playing in her shadow when I was little, pretending I could take those arms and wrap them around me. The way I wanted to now.

"Sarah Nita, are you watching? This is the plant we harvest for the yellow ocher color." She tells me we need at least three of such plants to dye the wool. But I am not thinking about that; I am thinking about my mother. How she smells of sheep and wool and wood smoke. How her hair is always smooth, the way a Navajo woman's hair should be. How her woolen dress is neat and clean, her leggings a soft red in the sunlight.

Just this morning she combed my hair with the stiff grass brush, untangling it and clucking her tongue. Now that I am twelve summers, she told me, I should be taking better care. She wondered how I could get so many tangles in my hair, and did I get up and race around the hogan while she was sleeping? That made Kaibah, my younger sister, laugh. *Her* hair is never in clumps in the morning, even though she has nine summers; *she* always remembers to bathe her face in snow in the winter so that her skin will be clear and smooth when she is grown.

But not me.

"My daughter! If you were a goat I would have to pull you by a little rope. Your thoughts keep wandering off!"

I duck my head, tugging at the plant before me and almost falling. If my mother asks me why my thoughts are like goats wandering about the mesa, I will have to tell her, *It is that bad news the traveler brought. About the* Bilagáana, *the white men, and how they are doing such strange and terrible things to our people. Burning our crops and hogans. Rounding up our people like animals and driving them away to some far place.*

"My daughter." Mother's voice is gentle but firm.

I say that if she will tell me a story while we are collecting plants, then I can listen better. I love her stories; when I listen, I feel I am sitting on a rug with bright colors beneath, with all the patterns clear and beautiful.

And so she begins the story of one of our Holy People who gave us weaving: "Once long ago Spider Woman saw how the poor people were naked and shivering, with no clothes to keep them warm, no rugs to lie on or lie under at night. She wondered if it would not be a good idea to help those sad humans to be happier."

"And to be warmer!" I interrupt, then clap my hand to my mouth.

My mother walks on to another plant, twisting it easily out of the earth. "So Spider Woman taught women how to card and spin wool, how to weave rugs of soft earth colors. She gave names to the spindle, every part of the loom, and told us always to spin toward the body, not away from it. That way the wool would be beautiful.

"But you know, my daughter, that you must always leave a little hole in your rugs."

I know that must be so, for if I did not, my thoughts would get all tangled up in the rug, like my hair at night, and I would become crazy, like someone with a dark wind inside of them. I didn't want *that* to happen!

Then Kaibah calls to us from far away. She is a small figure in front of our hogan, and I am angry at her for interrupting us. I want to keep listening to my mother's words, to hear her talk about our Holy People. Reluctantly, I gather up our plants and head for our hogans — one is Mother's, and the other is my aunt's. Both have shade houses nearby where we can keep cool on hot days. Beyond, I can see the fields where we harvest our corn, squash, pumpkins, and beans. Our brushwood corral is near the shade of some trees, to keep our sheep and goats cool.

I love walking home; I love how my moccasins make small hollows in the red dirt.

I close my ears against fearful words

Kaibah and I help Mother make the mutton stew that night. We put in some sagebrush leaves for flavoring, and I think I could almost eat the smell, it is so good. I help Mother grind corn for tomorrow, working the smooth oval stone against the corn kernels scooped in a broad rock — back and forth, smoothly, smoothly.

I never do anything smoothly. I am full of rushes, starts, quick jumps. To be still is very hard for me. Mother tells me I am like our brown and white goat who pokes her face through the hogan door, blinking at the darkness, curious and impatient.

Kaibah stirs the stew quietly, carefully. Father sits near the fire, with the rug pulled down over the door opening. Now it is the Time of the Parting of the Seasons; nights are cool, the wind is cool.

When my mother tells us to come to eat from the big pot, I sniff deeply. I *know* I could walk a day's journey just on that good scent! The grown-ups talk of corn, harvests, and the time of cold winds coming. I think, *We will always live like this, the way the Holy People mean us to live, planting pumpkins and squash, hunting deer in the hills, herding our sheep and goats. Nothing can change this.*

But Father speaks that terrible word again, the one I have heard too often lately — *Bilagáana.* "A man riding through today told me his crops were burned by the white men. He was all alone."

We wonder at that — to be a *Diné,* a Navajo, alone is like seeing one goose flying South. It would never happen.

My mother wonders where he was going, but Father does not know for certain. "He said some words about going farther west, where there would be no white men."

Mother snorts and says there is no place left on Earth without white men. They are like locusts settling everywhere. But Father reminds her that there is one safe place left — *tseyi* — the sacred canyon to the north. He has heard that some of our people are fleeing there to hide, and he has cousins there, family.

"We could go there, too," my father says, "if the soldiers — the men in blue — come for us." But he does not want to go there now, not with food stored for winter, not until he knows more about these men in blue.

I put my hands over my ears; I do not want to be rude, but if I can just keep those words *outside* my head, they will not harm us. Words can hurt — words can kill. They can cure sickness, or they can bring sickness down on you. *Don't you know that?* I want to shout. *If you talk about those bad white people, your words will pull them here.*

I think about winds

I wake in the darkness. Everything is black, except for the faint line of moonshine around the door rug. My father snores slightly while Mother breathes more softly. The fire has gone out. Kaibah is curled beside me, sleeping like a little fox in its den.

Outside, our dog, Silver Coat, is moving restlessly

and whining. Softly, I get up, pull back the rug, and go outside. Wolves? Coyotes?

The moon shines down on the trees near our hogan. Shadows splash the ground. When I hold my breath, I can almost hear the land breathing — a deep, silent sigh. I think it says, *You are the people I want to live on me — you* Diné. *You will care for me, like a mother for her child.*

Is the land as worried about the white men as we are? Does it wake in the night, afraid of what is coming?

My uncle Long Legs told me about the winds in our land, the *Dinetah* — how one comes from the West, one from the East, another from the North, and one from the South. "There is even a little wind that lives inside you, Sarah Nita. See the patterns on your fingertips?"

I stare at them now in the moonlight, though I cannot see the ripples I know are there. My neck prickles as I think, *There are inside winds and outside winds, but something . . . something.* I hate this shivery feeling on my neck; it has happened a few times before, and something bad always followed. My mother told me that her father, who was a great singer and healer, sometimes knew what was coming, just the way a dog scents something unseen. I wonder — is there a wind Uncle Long Legs never told me about, one that brings evil change?

Leaves sift down to the ground in a slight breeze, and I run inside to huddle close to my sister, my little fox.

I do not want my cousin to see me naked

It is warm today, the sun shining so hot on my shoulders that it feels as if I am standing too close to the fire.

"Can we bathe in the water hole today, Mother?" I ask as she sweeps the floor of our hogan with a sagebrush broom.

"Mmm," she answers, not attending to me, and I wonder if she is thinking about that man who rode past alone. Such a thing is a sign. If my mother sees a yellow bird, her face will light up. "A lucky day!" And she will sing all morning, sure that bad things are far away. So that man alone was an unlucky sign, something to worry and wonder about.

But I don't want to think about bad luck today. For me, "mmmm" means "yes," so beckoning to Kaibah, we run outside. My younger cousin, Shidezhi, is there, helping my aunt card wool in the shade of a tree. When she sees us, she asks if she can come, too. Aunt tells her it is all right, and taking her stiff grass hairbrush with her, Shidezhi follows us across the dry ground.

Today her older brother, Swift Pony, is watching all of our sheep, so we are free. Our moccasins fly over the earth, we are so happy to have time away from our chores — carding wool, grinding corn, cleaning the ground in or near the hogan, gathering firewood and fetching water.

When we get to the water hole, we see how low it is. In the spring, after the snows melt, it brims along the edges and ripples in the breeze. Now it is sunk into the orange-red rock, with little tufts of dried grass in the cracks.

Kaibah takes off her moccasins and hops, saying, "Ouch, ouch, ouch!" Then, "Oooh, ooh," when she puts her feet into the water.

We all pull off our dusty wool dresses, beating them with sticks to get out the dirt. There is only room for one person at a time in the water hole, so we wait while Kaibah rubs herself with gravel and ducks her head under the surface.

Shidezhi asks if our father is as worried as hers is. She says he never smiles these days; his mouth is like an upside-down bowl. I sigh that my father is the same.

So we make more noise than usual, splash higher than usual, giggle more than we would. And that is why we do not hear Swift Pony approaching from behind us.

"Aha! Naked girls in the sun! What a sight!" he crows, clapping his hands. His sister throws a rock at him, and I pull on my dress before I am dry. Suddenly, I am shy with that boy I've known all my life. And I do not want him to see my skin, to see the strange things that are happening to my body. Where my chest once was flat, now there are two bumps sticking out. My mother says that soon boys will look at me differently, that in time I will become a woman and have the *kinaaldá* ceremony.

That makes me shiver; I am not ready, not yet. I want things to stay the same and never change, but that cannot be. And I know I do not want Swift Pony to see me naked anymore.

I try to change my father's face

That night, when we cut open a pumpkin and roast it over the fire, I touch Father's arm. I have always been proud of him, how tall and straight he is, like a tree, and how his dark eyes look straight into mine. I like his little jokes and how he teases me, pulling slightly on my hair, pretending to be a squirrel scampering up my arm, searching for nuts in my hair. But today he is not teasing me, and he is not smiling. How can I get him to smile?

When I listen to my mother's stories, they make me feel that everything is right inside of me and outside. She tells me that I am like my grandfather, her father, who was a great storyteller. I do not know if she's right, but I do know that if I sit very quietly, sometimes a tale comes into my mind, like a bird flying into a hogan.

"Once," I begin, words and pictures floating into my head, "there was a child who was called Worried Girl. Do you know why she was called that?"

Father looks down at me and touches my nose. "Why, Sarah Nita?" At least he is listening now, instead of frowning into the fire.

"She was named Worried Girl because every day when she woke up, she did not see the smiles of her mother and father anymore. Her aunts and uncles had faces with clouds in them. Even the sheep looked worried, and the bad goats who tried to run away. It made her face frown; it made her forehead pucker up.

"She said to herself, *How can I make this worry go away? I want a new name!* She thought and thought, and one night when the moon was out, she heard an owl calling. 'Grandfather Owl,' she asked, 'tell me how I can drive the clouds from the faces of my aunts and uncles, of my father and mother.'

"Grandfather Owl hooted softly and beat his wings silently. But Worried Girl saw darkness moving in the trees. And he answered her, 'A song can put happiness into a person. A story can take away sorrow.'

"'Thank you, Grandfather Owl,' the girl replied, and she hurried back to her hogan.

"In the morning, Worried Girl got up, swept the hogan, and ground the corn. Whatever she did, she sang as she did it. The songs were like golden leaves drifting in the wind; her mother's face brightened; her father smiled. And though they did not smile *all* the time, Worried Girl learned that singing could push sorrow away, that telling stories could keep sadness outside the hogan. She earned a new name — The Girl Who Chased Away Sorrow."

Father sighs, pulling me close to his body. I can feel the heat coming out, and something like the dark stain of worry going away. "Your name should be that."

He does not say any more; we are quiet around the fire. But my mother's face is not so worried tonight, and

Kaibah gives me a special look, almost the way I used to look at my grandfather when he told a story. I never understood how he could remember all those words, all those chants. That is the way she looked at me.

We stuff bags with gold

All day we are harvesting corn — beating the dried ears with sticks and catching the kernels on sheepskins my mother spread out on the earth. It looks like gold lying in heaps on the animal skins. And my mother sings as she scoops up the kernels, putting them into sacks to keep for winter.

I sing softly with her, happy to be in the sun, putting golden corn into bags.

Mother looks small

The next morning Mother tells Kaibah and me to take the sheep to the low mesa near our hogan. Our family has decided that the sheep must be grazed as near to home as possible. They do not have to tell us why — we know.

My sister grins at me, happy to be outside this day —

in spite of everyone's worries about the *Bilagáana*. I thought I could get back at Swift Pony for sneaking up on us; maybe I could sneak up on him! When I pull open the brushwood gate of our corral, our dog rounds up the sheep, nipping at their heels.

Mother kneels by the fire outside, getting ready to dye some wool from the plants we'd gathered. "I will see you at sunset, my daughters," she calls, piling dry wood on the fire and readying the pot filled with water.

Suddenly, worry settles over me like a cloud. Mother looks small, as if she could be blown away by a cold wind. The hair rises along my neck, and I run back to bury my face in her wool dress that smells of smoke and sheep.

"Sarah Nita, what is wrong?" But I cannot find the words to tell her — even I don't know.

She waves her hand at me, not thinking of me but of the fire and when it will be ready to dye wool. It is hard to walk away, and I keep turning my head for one last look. My skin still prickles, frightening me, and Kaibah takes my hand as we walk. I guess my mouth looks like an upside-down bowl, too.

An evil wind comes

When we reach the top of the low mesa, nothing has changed. Yellow aspen leaves flutter in the wind. Sheep's heels click against stones. I love the soft tearing and munching sound of the animals eating dry grass. Kaibah hums to herself and braids a rope out of yucca leaves she's brought with her.

I do not know how long we stay there, watching the sheep. From time to time, I run after our bad goat and swat her on the rump with a knotted rope. She is a mischief-maker, and the sheep always try to follow her. After the second or third time the goat tries to escape, Kaibah calls to me.

She stands at the edge of the mesa, her hair blowing in the wind. She points to the place of the rising sun, where a red cloud smokes up from the earth. What is it? Why does it make me shiver? Trees bend, I try to speak, but my lips are numb. Grabbing a piece of brush, I try to sweep that evil wind away before it can bring harm to us.

Kaibah calls, "What is that cloud, Sister?" But I cannot answer, and I open and shut my mouth silently like a caught fish.

Our dog is crazy

Kaibah holds her hand out to me. Somehow, I move over the dry ground. The sheep are still grazing, but the dog's ruff is raised as he looks toward the red cloud. When I grab my sister's hand, we look toward home.

"Why are you afraid, Sarah Nita? What's wrong?"

Down below are the two hogans and the small figures of our family, working. Smoke rises from my mother's fire. But beyond the hogans, that red cloud comes closer, closer.

"Is it a storm?" Kaibah asks in a voice so thin, it is like spider silk.

Out of the dust come horses with blue figures on them. Something gleams in the sun, like light on mica. I hear a *pop!* Then another, then the sound of someone screaming. Oh, let it not be our mother!

Together we race for the path that will take us down to them. But the dog is faster than we are, darting ahead and blocking the narrow way down. Lips pulled back, he snarls at us.

"Silver Coat!" I shout at him. "Get away!" But he does not obey me and stands in front, baring his teeth. Kaibah tries to run past, but he jumps forward and nips her leg. Something pounds inside my body, and I hit Silver Coat with the knotted rope. I have to get down that path! The dog flinches, but does not move, growling so loudly and fiercely that I am afraid he will bite me, too.

That terrible scream comes again, like a *chindi,* a ghost, near a death hogan, and we cover our ears. Huddled together, afraid of the people in blue and afraid of the dog, we don't know where to go. Below, red flames leap from our hogans, and Kaibah groans. Men in blue, mounted on horses, round up our horses and drive them and our family ahead over the land.

Again we try to get to the path, but Silver Coat plants his feet on the earth and will not move. We cannot go forward, we cannot go back. Kaibah opens her mouth and lets out a sound like a ghost crying, and the dog howls with her.

Silver Coat lets us pass

How long does it take for evil to come, to break everything you know, like that evil giant of long ago who smashed huge trees and boulders? I wish Monster-Slayer were here, right now, to save us and kill those blue soldiers. But He lived in the Long Ago Time, not now, and we can only stand on the mesa, watching our family become smaller and smaller like birds flying out of sight, until they disappear behind a rise in the land.

Sometime later, when the sun is low in the sky, Silver Coat steps forward and bows to me, waving his tail. Kaibah will not go near him, afraid he has gone crazy. Gently, I hold out a hand to him, and he wags his tail. Then I know; he was protecting us, and now that the soldiers are far away, he does not have to guard us anymore.

Holding our arms across our chests, Sister and I herd the sheep down from the mesa. I think that when terrible things happen, you keep doing everyday things. The sun shines, the leaves blow, and we herd our sheep.

We don't talk, walking slowly at first, then running ahead of the sheep to our hogans. At the edge of camp, we stop, hands clamped to our mouths. There is a bitter, choking smell from the burning hogans; flames and black smoke pour into the sky. Things are scattered all over the ground — mother's metal pot, a sack of food, a bone tool, two sheepskins.

The sheep clatter over the ground as Silver Coat rounds them up, driving them into the corral. Kaibah remembers to run over, close the brushwood gate, and come back to me. Even though I know they are gone, I can't help calling out, "Mother, Father? Aunt and Uncle, Cousins?" as if they could answer from far away. But there are no voices, just the evil crackling of the fire.

I hear a wounded animal sound that makes me turn around to see where it is coming from. It isn't Kaibah, it isn't the dog. It is me.

Kaibah tells me to hide

Sister tugs on my hand, saying the soldiers might come back, and we must hide. Before we leave, I grab the sheepskins and the sack of food from the ground. Some other girl is doing these things, not I — some other person is thinking about food, about shelter and sleeping. The girl that is Sarah Nita is hiding deep inside, saying over and over to herself, *Where is my mother? Where is Father? Are you alive?*

Our things bump against us as we run away from the burning hogans to a stretch of junipers on a low hill. Is it far enough away? Is any place far enough away from what has happened?

While Silver Coat stands guard, we crawl in under the shelter of two large junipers growing together. It feels safe behind the green wall of pine needles. I remember that this is a place Kaibah and I played in when we were younger, making dolls out of cornstalks and pieces of old cloth. It was a safe place, a happy place.

Arms wrapped around each other, we pull the sheepskins over us. I do not know if I am even hungry or tired; I am just a body — a shivering body.

I hit Silver Coat

When Kaibah stirs beside me and the dog noses my leg, I keep my eyes shut. If I stay very still and do not open my eyes, maybe everything will be the same. Soon Mother will call to us to get up; soon Swift Pony will come to tease me. But my stomach grumbles, and a cold wind stirs my hair. Kaibah moans, rubs her face with one sooty hand, and sits up. All the cool air rushes in when she pushes back the sheepskins.

"Sister?" Her voice is cracked and frightened.

I tell her that we are still here, near our home, that I am with her, and we will be all right. But my lips are trembling, so that the words come out all wrong, and Kaibah cannot understand me. We creep out from under the juniper branches into air that feels sharp and dangerous, where the blue sky is too big. Walking hunched over, I make myself go up to the smoldering hogans. When Silver Coat lifts his head and howls, I hit him on the ear. He runs away, and Kaibah says, "Sarah Nita! He did nothing wrong."

I cannot tell her what I am thinking: *No one can cry, not even the dog. If we are to survive this evil time, we must be brave.*

I wait for words inside

I feel as if aspen leaves are fluttering in the middle of my body. If I do not hold myself together, like a blanket bound tight with rope, I will fall into pieces. The only thing I can do is to pretend to be brave, like my father going off on a raid. Standing straight and tall, I touch the white shell necklace Mother gave me, the shell that is sacred to our Holy Person, Changing Woman. I remember how She gave birth to the twin heroes who killed the monsters that were harming our people. I remember how brave She was, how She cared for the *Diné*. But, still — still, I am trembling inside.

"Sister?"

Kaibah jumps, grabbing my arm. Suddenly, words pour out of her like a summer rain rushing down a canyon. I think our fear kept us silent before. What will we do, and where are Father and Mother, and should we follow them? she asks. Maybe we should try to catch up with the soldiers and then we would all be together, but then we would be prisoners, she gasps.

When I put my hand on her shoulder, she stops. It is too dangerous to follow them, I say, and we don't know where they are going or what is in the minds of the blue soldiers. We are only two girls — two brave girls, I remind her — who cannot fight against the blue men on horses.

"Then where will we go?" she wails, kneeling on the ground.

My mother, if you were here, what would you answer? Tell me what to do!

I kneel on the ground beside my sister, waiting for words to come, waiting the way I used to in front of our hogan, looking for the first sight of Father coming home from a raid.

You have family in tseyi. *The tall walls will hide you. Go there.*

Suddenly, the words are inside. And I think it is the voice of my mother, helping me to stop trembling, helping me to be brave.

"*Tseyi.*" The word pops out.

Holding tight to our dog, Kaibah gives me that look again, just like the time I told the story of The Girl Who Chased Away Sorrow. She thinks I know what to do, that I will take care of things. So I must pretend to know. I remind her that Father said the canyon was a little over a week's journey away, north and toward the setting sun, and that we have family there. As long as we keep the place where the sun rises beside our right shoulders, we will find it.

My words fall like pebbles into the water hole — now I must act as if I believe them.

I try to get the knife

Somehow we make ourselves move past the yawning mouths of those two smashed doorways — the place where we sang songs, ate our meals, snuggled close to our family on cold winter nights. I have rolled up the two sheepskins and am carrying them on my back. Kaibah picks up Mother's gourd outside her hogan, finding a sack of dried pumpkin that was tossed aside by the fire. She grabs a bag of ground corn, too.

"Here's Mother's pot, Sister! And look, her flint!" Triumphantly, she waves it at me.

But I am thinking of something else right now, afraid of what I must do. Slowly I go up to Mother's hogan. If I can just reach through the door . . . no one has died here. I did count how many were led away by the soldiers — six for our family, fourteen for the men in blue.

I know where she kept her knife, the one Father brought back from a raid; it was on a ledge to the right of the smashed doorway. We will need it to cut up animals we hunt on the way, and to protect us from puma and wolves. Slowly, I stretch out my arm to the dark opening. Blackness flows out of it and a terrible smell.

"Aiyee!" I shout, and take to my heels. Running, I see nothing but a blur of red, blue, and brown. Something runs beside me — I do not know what. And it pants and breathes and whispers.

We cannot run anymore

Silver Coat stops first, his tongue lolling. Even though the wind is cool today, sweat pours off our bodies, soaking our dresses. The dog's tail drags in the dust, and suddenly, I feel the weight and heat of the sheepskins against my back. Kaibah complains that the gourd and pot have been knocking against her waist, hurting her.

We collapse on the ground, pouring water into our throats. I know we should save more for later, but we are so thirsty!

"Don't forget Silver Coat." Kaibah trickles a little water into his open mouth, but it is not enough, and he begs with his eyes and waving tail.

When we are cooled down, we mix some of the cornmeal with water. Every time I swallow, I see our hogan, I see my mother, Father, Aunt, and Uncle, Swift Pony, and Shidezhi. Then my throat closes, and I can't eat anymore.

Rising, we go on, brushing past dried grass, rabbitbrush, and prickly pear cactus. I know that if we are very hungry, we can always roast the cactus in a fire, pull out the thorns, and eat it. I remember to look up and check the position of the sun. It is directly overhead, and where it rises is beside my right shoulder. We are going the right way.

We are like hunted rabbits

The longer we walk, the more afraid I am. I think I hear *chindi,* ghosts, crying in the wind; I keep looking over my shoulder for soldiers. When Kaibah starts and dashes behind a tree, I follow. Crouched in the safe shade, we stay for a while, until our hearts stop thumping. We are like *gah* that boys hunt — rabbits darting from side to side, zigzagging to get away from their killers.

We find a hiding place

We keep to the shadows of junipers and piñon pines. My head is buzzing like a bee tree, and my breath sounds like someone crying. I am trying to be brave, like a Navajo warrior or like Changing Woman, but I don't feel brave. What will we do if we see other soldiers? Every tree is a place to hide; every shadow is a place to lie down in. But soon the shadows are longer, darker — *like blood* — and I turn uphill, grabbing Sister's hand. The flat land feels too dangerous now, and we crawl up the pine-covered slopes, the dog just behind.

"What are you looking for, Sister?" Kaibah pants beside me, the metal pot making a lonely creaking sound.

"I will know when I find it," I tell her.

Finally, near the top of the hill, I see an old piñon pine with its branches drooping to the ground. On my knees, I pull Kaibah in after me, and we curl up under the branches with our arms around each other.

Together we get warm enough so that we can stop shivering. Sitting up, Kaibah brushes the hair from her face, offering me cornmeal from the sack. But it is so hard to swallow that dry food with only a small drink of water from the gourd. *My mother, where are you now? My father, what are they doing to you and to all of my family?*

Now the sun is setting, and the pictures in my mind are so terrifying that I look at the ground. Ants are carrying tiny pieces of food back to their nests. I wish I could be as small as one, hidden in the earth.

Different kinds of pictures and words begin to float inside of me. "Once in the Long Ago Time there were ant people," I begin.

"Maybe, somewhere behind these red hills, there still are some ant people alive. I know," I say to Sister's look of disbelief, "that they lived in the Second World before people came to be."

The words calm my breathing, calm the pounding in my chest. "But maybe two of the ant people crept through those hollow reeds so long ago because they wanted to see the sun in the glittering world. And unseen, they crept up here and had many beautiful, smart children.

"The task of those children is to guide lost *Diné* children and keep them safe."

Kaibah leans against me and sighs.

"We can't see them, but they're there. Just beyond the ridge on that hill and in a hollow over there. They will dim the sight of the white men when they come looking for us. They will help us scurry as fast as they do to hiding places along the way, and to our final hiding place in *tseyi*."

The words hang in the air like sweet wood smoke from home. Kaibah pats my arm as we unroll the sheepskins and pull them up to our chins. Darkness comes, and I dream of swift and clever ant children guiding us, keeping us safe.

I dare to make a fire

When I wake, it is still dark. Silver Coat is lying on top of our legs, and I have to ease myself out from under him. But no one stirs; my sister and the dog are too tired.

Walking around the hillside, I gather some firewood, for I have decided that today we will have a fire and cook corn mush. After I have a pile, I make a smaller nest of dried tinder to catch the spark of shredded cedar bark and pine needles.

I thank Changing Woman that we have a metal pot to cook in and cornmeal from home. When I strike the flint, the spark catches in the tinder. I blow on it and drop it onto the wood, jumping when a cold nose pokes my elbow.

"Silver Coat!" I shout. "Don't do that!" But he bows to me, stretching and wagging his tail, and I have to forgive him.

Kaibah crawls out of her sheepskin and crouches by the fire as I fan it with a piece of bark. She sighs, holding her hands out to the flame. She tells me our sleeping tree is so secret and hidden that the ant children must have helped us. I pat her hand, glad that she is with me, that I am not alone.

But Kaibah still looks to me as if I were the grown-up; I know better. Anything can happen on our way to *tseyi,* and if we die — caught by animals or soldiers — no one will ever know.

I remember storing the corn

When Kaibah and I scoop the cooked corn mush onto pieces of bark, we remember to thank the Holy People for it. I think about that day when we put golden corn into bags for winter. *This* is some of that corn; something my mother touched. Will it bring us good luck?

We see blue soldiers

As soon as we are done, Kaibah and I scrape dirt over the fire. Just as the last wisp of smoke sails up, Kaibah stops moving, and the dog points his nose toward the flat land below.

Sister motions to me; then I hear it, too — the pounding of hooves. Quickly, we head for our shelter of last night, dragging everything under the branches and lying flat. But being so close to the earth, it is hard to see; thick grass and junipers make it hard to see. Holding tight to our dog's coat, I peer through the branches, trying to see what is happening. My heart pounds so that I feel sick. Kaibah's eyes are squeezed shut, and her lips are moving. Is she praying for safety?

The sound of galloping stops; I see a flash of blue below, and hear loud voices — thick, harsh sounds. I am so afraid that my stomach clenches in, and I think I will be sick. *Oh, ant people, dim the sight of the blue soldiers, keep us hidden like ants in the sand!*

"Kmmrr . . ." comes from below.

Someone answers in a voice that lashes like a whip. Kaibah grabs my hand, squeezing so tight, I almost cry out.

A horse whinnies, someone shouts, and the galloping starts up again, growing fainter and fainter. I dare to raise my head, then my body, so I can see through the branches — soldiers moving fast over the red land, away from us. They are heading toward the rising sun, not the direction we are going in.

All we can do is press our hands to our mouths, willing that corn mush to stay inside until we are calm enough to go on.

Changing Woman will show us the way

We finish the last of our water after the sun sets, then we curl up to sleep under two juniper trees. We did not go far this day, too frightened by the sight of those blue soldiers. I am trying not to worry; listening for my mother's voice inside. But there are no words — only wind in the junipers, and when we put our heads down, my throat feels like a gully in the summer heat.

The next day we set off with the rising sun on our

right. I do not know if we are heading straight for *tseyi,* but I touch my white shell necklace and pray that Changing Woman will show us the way and help us find water. For now our gourd is almost empty, and my mouth feels like dust. We walk and walk, our heels making half circles in the red dirt. Kaibah does not say a word, just presses her lips together. Is she thinking of Mother's words? "Remember, the *Diné* are strong. A *Diné* girl does not complain."

The blue sky hurts my eyes, and the red of the mesas reminds me of home. Grabbing Kaibah's hand, I hold as tight as I can. She squeezes back but does not say a word.

Silver Coat finds water

When the sun is high overhead, we stop and eat some dry cornmeal. It feels like sand in my throat. Kaibah is trying to swallow, but she chokes on the dusty food and spits some out of her mouth. Suddenly, Silver Coat barks and dashes out of sight.

"Soldiers?" I mouth to Sister, but she tells me that was a happy bark, not a warning one. Running around a thicket of bushes, we see something sparkling in the light. Water! Silver Coat is standing in a stream, lapping as fast as he can.

We tear off our dusty wool dresses and wade in beside him. But first, I scan the landscape for blue soldiers, for the telltale smoke from a fire. There is nothing.

"Cold!" Kaibah says softly, filling the gourd. She puts her face into the water, drinks deeply, and I do the same. Splashing water over our heads, we scoop up gravel from the bottom and rub the dirt off our bodies. Even though the water numbs our skin and makes us gasp, we grin, watching a brown streak swirl away. I remember Swift Pony, how he surprised me the last time we bathed, and my eyes squeeze shut. Where is he now? Will I ever know?

The days go on forever

The days blur together like rain washing down a hillside. One day Silver Coat catches a squirrel, and we steal it from him to roast over the fire. We have to spit out the fur again and again. It has a smoky, charred taste, but Silver Coat doesn't seem to mind! One day we find water again and fill the gourd. Another day we see soldiers in the distance and hide on a hillside, only coming out at night to walk. Sister reminds me that the ant people are keeping us hidden. The other days have no markers, just sweat, tired feet, and huddling together at night under our sheepskins.

Kaibah holds up her hand to the light. "Eight days, Sister. When will we get to *tseyi*?"

I am proud of her; she has only complained once on our journey, when her feet hurt. I will not tell her that I'm not sure where we are, that I don't know what we will do if we don't reach the canyon soon.

I listen for my mother's voice, to tell me if we are on the right path, but there are no words inside. If only she were with me right now, to tell me she needs a rope to lead me by! I would be so good, so quiet, so calm.

Tseyi!

Scrabbling up a hill the next morning, Kaibah stops at the top and points. "Look!"

Below are tall trees with white scaly bark — the kind that grow near water. We skid down the slope, Silver Coat running beside us, and see a blackened field ahead. Kaibah stops, says one word, "Soldiers," and turns to go back. But I kneel by the field and touch the earth; it is cold, the cornstalks are long dead. Do they belong to the people of the canyon?

Together, holding hands, we come to a wide, shallow stream with cottonwoods thick along its edges. Quietly, we walk beside the stream, always keeping to the shadow of the trees. But we have to follow the water; it could lead us to the people who planted those fields. As we round a bend in the river, sudden tall pink walls rise up to the blue sky. They had been hidden by the trees before.

"*Tseyi!*"

"*Tseyi.*" I whisper this time, like a word from a sacred song to keep us from evil.

We have come to the end of our journey, and somewhere inside those walls are our people.

The walls look bloody

Suddenly, my bones feel strong. How my feet fly over the earth! Kaibah races beside me as the canyon walls soar upward — a warm pink with long black streaks down them, as if a terrible flood had marked them, or fire.

When we slow to catch our breath, Kaibah gives me a quick, sideways look. "Sarah Nita? It looks like a monster was killed here, and those marks are his dried blood."

I shake my head and cannot answer. A terrible thought pierces me — what if what we've left behind is safer than what we've run to? And what if there are no people inside the canyon?

It is too quiet

We walk deeper into the canyon; our poor skinny dog's tail is between his legs, and I wonder if he is as afraid as we are. We let him keep the last squirrel he caught, so he is not starving — not yet. Sparkling in the afternoon sunlight, the river runs through the sandy floor of the canyon. But where is everyone? There should be women filling their water gourds. There should be children herding their sheep to the river, but there is no one.

Kaibah tugs on my hand, pointing to an old cornfield beside the stream. The stems stick up into the sky, and I shout, my voice banging off the canyon walls. Silver Coat sits on his haunches and howls at the noise as Sister clamps her hands over her ears.

"Hush!"

I did not mean to shout, but the sight of that cornfield is so good — someone lives here, somewhere.

Another night alone

Though we walk until it is almost dark, we see no one. The sun leaves the canyon early, making dark shadows on the bottom while light still lies along the top of its walls. It makes me dizzy to look up, as if I am standing at the edge of a high cliff about to fall down.

Kaibah wonders, "Maybe the people live farther in, hiding from the soldiers, Sarah Nita."

I am looking for a rock overhang to shelter us from the cold tonight. "Maybe we will find them tomorrow," I whisper, afraid to make too much noise.

When we find a place where the rock wall bulges out, we unroll our sheepskins and curl up again to sleep on our own.

Someone puts his arms around me

The next day is bright, clear, and cold. The sunlight has not reached the bottom of the canyon yet, and I think it must be colder here than it is at the top. After we thank Changing Woman and the ant people for helping us to reach *tseyi,* Kaibah and I build a small fire for warmth.

The cornmeal has been used up, and all we have are dried pieces of hard pumpkin. But when we soak them in water in Mother's pot and stew them over the fire, they taste of home. I am trying to be brave, to remind myself that a *Diné* girl is strong, but that taste of pumpkin makes me cry.

Suddenly, Sister jabs me in the ribs. With no sound, no warning, people surround us — an old man with gray hair, a worn tunic, and leggings, and an old woman carrying a water gourd. A girl and an older boy stare at us as I wipe my eyes on my dress.

"Yah-ta-hey," the old woman calls.

"Yah-ta-hey, Grandmother," we greet her.

"Why are you crying, children? Where have you come from?" she asks.

I tell her that the soldiers took our family away, that my sister and I have been journeying from the South to *tseyi,* and that my father has clan here. Grandmother exclaims how brave we are, making the journey on our own, and how sad she is about our family. Solemnly, she asks which clan we belong to, and I answer that we were born to our mother's clan, the Salt People, and we were born for our father's clan, the Bitter Water People.

"They did not escape here, did they?" Sister interrupts, naming each person in our family.

Shaking his head sadly, the old man steps forward and hugs me. "Your father is not here, but we are from the same clan. Call me Grandfather, and my wife Grandmother." He says many long words about who is related to whom, but all I can see is the big smile on the old woman's face and the grins of the children. I am too sad to smile, and so is Kaibah, but at least we are not alone. Not anymore. And I think how lucky we are that out of all the people who could be in the canyon, the first ones we meet are from my father's clan.

Even Silver Coat looks happy, wagging his tail and going from person to person in greeting. He licks Grandfather's and Grandmother's knees, feet, and anything else he can reach. Grandfather jokes, "That dog of yours is from the Pouring Water clan and he's pouring water all over my knees!"

We find their hogan

When they tell us to follow them, we walk farther into the canyon. Kaibah's head droops, and her moccasins scuff over the dried grass. I take one hand, and one of the grandchildren, the little girl with the golden thread of yarn around her hair, takes the other.

"I am Partridge Girl, and my brother is High Jumper." I take a quick look at his long legs and thin face; he reminds me of Swift Pony, my cousin.

Grandfather talks in a low, quiet voice; the soldiers were near the canyon a while ago, driving away their sheep, setting fire to their cornfields. Some of their people have even been caught outside the canyon and taken away by the soldiers.

"The minds of white men are filled with dark winds," High Jumper says in a bitter voice.

Grandfather nods and reminds his grandson that the *Bilagáana* have some plan that we do not understand, that we are being punished for raiding their ranches and taking sheep and horses. High Jumper strides ahead and slaps one hand against his leg, spitting out that now that the white men have burned our fields and stolen our sheep, the *Diné* are beginning to starve.

Grandmother does not agree or disagree, and when I look at the lines in her thin face, I wonder how much they have to eat. Will we be a burden to them? But before I can ask, we stop near the face of a steep cliff. In front of it is a low, round hogan — like home. Grandmother tells us that there is still some food stored high in the rock face, and points to a nearby corral with some sheep and goats inside.

"Goat's milk!" Kaibah looks hungrily at the animals. Grandmother pats her head, saying we will have some to drink later. When she pulls back the door blanket, High Jumper motions me to sit down by the fire. I feel as if my mother were hugging me close; the warm darkness of the hogan, the solid walls, and the blankets on the ground circle around me like arms.

A *beast is breathing in the back*

They feed us cornmeal mixed with goat's milk, heated over the fire in a metal pot like Mother's. Grandfather asks for the story of our journey, and Kaibah tells him part of it, I the rest. They seem to think we have done something brave and astonishing, coming here all on our own. I wonder if I am brave, if I am becoming the kind of *Diné* girl my mother would be proud of.

More people come into the hogan, a short, sturdy woman with a baby on her back. I learn that she is called Mexican Woman because she was born to a Navajo slave and her Mexican owner. She and her mother escaped and came back to our lands, the *Dinetah,* when she was still a girl. I think, *This is a brave person, this woman, whom we will call Aunt.*

When Kaibah and I look at her baby in the cradle board, and wave our fingers before her little face, someone coughs harshly on the other side of the fire. I thought that it was a heap of blankets there, but now I see it is a man under the coverings. Eyes closed, he makes terrible sounds when he breathes — long, sucked-in breaths, and then a slow sigh going out.

Kaibah clutches my hand as Grandfather explains that his son, Yellow Earrings, was shot by the soldiers a moon ago. Mexican Woman is his wife, and I watch her kneel beside him, holding up the bowl of mush to his lips.

Now the hogan feels dangerous to me with that Half-Alive Man breathing and sighing in the corner, and I know Kaibah feels the same, for she never lets go of my hand.

We feel like human beings again

Soon more people come into the hogan from outside —
High Jumper and Partridge Girl's mother and father.
He is called Man with a Lamb Hat because he al-
ways wears such a hat, and his wife is Slim Woman.
But we will call him Uncle, and she will be our other
aunt.

"You must have a bath, children, and be cleansed and
have your hair brushed," she tells us.

I remember once Father telling me about a woman
who had escaped from the New Mexicans. When she returned to her family, they did not know her at first and
had to have a special ceremony for her — to drive off ill
luck and make her part of the family again. I wonder if
that is what my aunt wants.

We are shy about taking off our clothes, even though
Grandmother wraps us in blankets. When Grandmother whips up yucca suds in a clay bowl, tears come
to my eyes, for that is what Mother used to do for us.
Pouring it over our heads, Grandmother rubs our hair
until we are clean.

Soon, we are clothed in other wool dresses (neater
than ours), and Aunt uses the stiff grass brush first on

Kaibah (who squeezes her eyes shut in pain), then on me. I yelp only once.

"Now you can feel like human beings again." Grandmother tells Aunt to give us some dried peaches soaked in water. Aunt passes the clay bowl to her son, High Jumper, who hands it to me with a shy smile.

"Welcome to our family."

Kaibah sighs, leaning her head against my shoulder. The part that Aunt made in her hair is like a clean road over the middle of her head. We have traveled so far! I only hope this is the end of our journeying for a long time, that we can stay here until the crazy white men decide to let our people return to our lands. Then we will go back and find our family again. I vow this: *I will look for you, my mother, until I find you; I will look for you, my father, until I find you, and my aunt, uncle, and cousins. We will be together again.*

Our first night inside

When it is dark in the hogan, when the stories are over and everyone is fed, people roll up in blankets to sleep by the fire. We spread out our sheepskins, and Kaibah and I curl together. But I don't look across the fire or listen to that harsh breathing of Grandfather's wounded son.

With my face near Kaibah's clean hair, I remember something Mother used to say: "Only a foolish person borrows trouble from the days to come." But I know from what Grandfather has said that even *tseyi* is not as safe as it once was; the soldiers have already been here, and they could come again.

Starlight, Aunt's baby, is making soft snuffling sounds as she nurses. She is so new, only born in the last moon. The sounds of her nursing cover up the other sounds I am trying not to hear; so I let sleep come like a friend, this night, instead of an enemy I must watch.

Aunt lets me help with her baby

The next day my aunt gives Kaibah the stiff grass brush to comb the tangles from our hair. "Just like our mother!" Kaibah says happily, brushing my hair.

While Grandfather and High Jumper go off to find firewood and Slim Woman milks the goat, my aunt tells me I can help with her baby. She asks Kaibah and me to find soft cliffrose bark to shred up and put under the baby's bottom.

When we find some, we peel off long strips and race back over the crackling grass; it is covered with frost, and the air is thin and cold in my nose. I can hardly believe it was warm enough to bathe in a stream a few days ago.

Before I duck through the hogan's door, I look up at the gray sky between the canyon walls. I wonder if somewhere my mother is looking up at the same sky and wondering where I am, too.

Inside the warm hogan, I watch Aunt unwrap Starlight, taking the soiled lining and throwing it out the door. Then I can hold the baby and play with her. I smile into her dark, surprised eyes. I think she likes moving her hands and arms with the air flowing up under her little woolen shirt. Kaibah makes a soft pile of shredded cliffrose bark and puts it beside the cradle board covered with deerskin.

"My husband made it in Harvest Time, before she was born," Aunt explains as she begins to wrap a long strip of warm cloth around her baby. When she gets near her bottom, Aunt tucks the soft bark inside the cloth wrappings and continues winding up to Starlight's neck. Then she is ready to tuck her into the cradle board.

Kaibah wants to play with her, but Aunt shakes her head; it is time for sleep, and we must be quiet. Soon the baby's eyelids close, and Aunt holds her up so that her husband can see. When his eyes flicker open and his lips move, his wife says, "Yes, it's Starlight, your daughter."

I think her smile will be like a patch of sunshine on little corn, making him grow stronger and taller. But his eyes shut, he sinks back into that dark place he lives in, and Aunt's face clouds over.

Kaibah and I race outside where we can be loud, shouting and running beside the river with our dog to leave Half-Alive Man behind.

I am still afraid

We have chores to do now in the mornings, Kaibah and I. We get fresh cliffrose bark for the baby and throw the old, used bark far from the hogan. High Jumper always goes with his father to gather firewood, for it is cold all day long now. Before Kaibah, Partridge Girl, and I leave to water the animals in the river, Aunt fusses over us.

"Wrap up well in these blankets; it is the Time of the Great Wind, children." I remember how my mother always wrapped blankets around us during this time, and my chest feels heavy when Aunt snugs the blanket under my chin. "If you hear anyone shouting a warning, come straight back here at once."

The lookouts on the canyon rim will warn us if they see soldiers coming. But how can we live like this, always looking over our shoulders, wondering when the soldiers will come next?

When we come back to the hogan for stewed pumpkin, Grandfather tells us that other families are hiding deeper in the canyon, some in hogans, some in brushwood shelters they built after fleeing here. And though the storage bins higher up in the rock walls still have some dried corn and pumpkins, I worry about how much is left, worry if we have done the right thing in coming here.

When it is our turn to dip our fingers into the pot, we only do it a few times, for there is never enough to really fill our bellies. If only the white men hadn't burned the corn and wheat outside the canyon! No one ever complains of the extra mouths to feed, but it hurts to see how thin Grandmother's wrists are when she reaches for the pot, to see the hollows in High Jumper's face — just like those in my sister's cheeks. Our dog is skinny, too, though I think he is catching squirrels in the canyon. I saw him one morning with a furry tail hanging out of his mouth, and Grandfather joked, "I was wrong. He is not from the Pouring Water clan, he is from the Hairy Lips clan!"

In spite of the soldiers, in spite of our worry, we can still makes jokes.

We play the string game

On a night when the wind blows cold, making the door rug flap and the flames stream sideways, Partridge Girl picks up a sack near the wall. I can't see what she is taking out, but when she returns, she sits cross-legged near Kaibah. Quickly, surely, she loops her fingers through a tied length of brown yarn.

"Stars in the sky," Aunt calls from her place by the fire.

Partridge Girl nods and holds out the weblike shape to Kaibah. Sister looks solemn, as if she's never played the string game before, but I know better. She is even swifter than me and knows many shapes. Hesitantly, she takes the yarn off her friend's fingers. Then, faster than I can see, she weaves a new pattern, yarn going over, under, and behind her fingers.

"You are fast!" says Partridge Girl, struggling to lift the yarn from Sister's hand.

Grandmother laughs, as Aunt does, with Starlight's head bobbing against her. For a moment, it seems as if the blue soldiers coming, the capture of my family, and our flight here is like something from a fever dream.

Then the fire sputters, the sick man coughs, and I am back again, in someone else's hogan without my family.

What if the soldiers come?

One morning after we have been in *tseyi* for almost a moon, thick snow swirls down from a gray sky. It falls on the ledges of the canyon, turning the green pines white, and it bites my flesh, so I tuck my hands under the blanket. High Jumper is keeping me company today as we guard the sheep, while Kaibah is helping Aunt with Starlight.

"What will we do if the soldiers come again, High Jumper?" I ask. "Where will we go?"

First, he points to a dark smudge on top of one of the canyon walls. "That is the lookout, to warn us if soldiers return. And there are hiding places deeper in the canyon that no *Bilagáana* knows about. There is a high rock farther in where our people could climb to the top, if we need to." He says that we could then pull up the notched tree trunk ladders so no soldiers could follow.

That does not calm me! A high rock we could retreat to in the Time of the Great Wind? And how would we get Half-Alive Man there? There is also a home of the Ancient Ones, High Jumper says, not too far away.

Just this morning, Grandfather set off down the canyon to prepare a tree ladder to that rock house in the canyon wall, in case the soldiers return. I am afraid of ghosts and ghost sickness in that old house but will not tell High Jumper that.

Suddenly he says over his shoulder, "I will protect you." How can a boy of thirteen summers protect me from ghosts? He gives me a quick sideways glance, and I wonder why he's talking to me this way. I run after the sheep, shouting louder than I usually do, as I drive them to the river. I wish, the way I do every day, that I were home again, in my own hogan, with my own mother, father, and family.

I see strange pictures on the rock

A few days later, Kaibah, Partridge Girl, and I break the ice on the river's edge to fill our gourds. Partridge Girl has given Sister a piece of golden yarn to bind her hair, too, and they look a little like sisters. High Jumper is ahead of us, jumping from one foot to another, trying to keep warm in the biting wind. I see how he got his name, with his great long legs like some wading bird's, and the way he can leap up into the air. Suddenly, he calls to us to follow and darts alongside the river.

Following him, we keep away from the ice crackling its edges. Besides, Grandfather told me to be careful of the river, to watch out for the sand that sucks you down. We pass a brushwood shelter with smoke coming out of the top, and High Jumper waves to a boy outside.

Soon High Jumper stops, pointing up at the pink canyon wall dotted with small green pines covered with snow. My breath smokes in the air, and Kaibah pulls her blanket tighter around her. At first I cannot see what he's pointing to, then I see: strange stick figures on the wall over my head — a bird, a man with a flute, a round circle. When I ask High Jumper what they are, he tells me they are something the Ancient Ones put on *tseyi*'s walls. He likes the pictures, but some people are afraid of them.

They remind me of the pictures of the *Yeis,* the Holy People, that my grandfather put in his sand paintings when he was asked to cure a sick person.

"I am not afraid of them," Partridge Girl says in a high voice, standing close to my sister.

Why should we be frightened, unless there are still ghosts in the canyon? Grandfather says over and over there are no ghosts here. But when I turn away from the painted wall, my skin prickles, and both girls hold tight to my hands. Even our dog walks with his tail between his legs. I stumble on a clump of grass when I remember — this is the way my skin felt that terrible day on the mesa at home, when that wind came and changed everything.

Is some evil wind coming here, too?

How white people came to be

The last few days have been so cold that we have all huddled inside the hogan, close to the fire. Grandfather has been telling stories, about First Man and Woman and how the *Diné* were made. My favorite is how the horse was created, with lightning in his ears, black coal for his coat, stars for his eyes, and streaks of rain in his mane. But when it came to the poor donkey, only the drab color gray was left for his coat and thunder for his voice.

When Grandfather tells a story, his eyes glisten and he sits straighter, like a man of thirty summers instead of the sixty he says he has.

His words spark pictures inside of me, as if someone holds lit tinder to kindling. "I think that when our dog was created, the Holy People told him to always do things in twos. When he barks, it is always twice."

Kaibah puts in that when he sneezes, it is always two times.

"And when our bad goat ran away, he chased her back to the hogan and bit her two times on each back leg."

Grandmother laughs and says softly "Twice." The words bring us together, just the way the yarn in the string game makes patterns that link our fingers.

Half-Alive Man speaks

While we tell stories, I try not to look across the fire at that heap of blankets that is a person. Not once have I heard him say more than two words. Except this time.

High Jumper wonders if First Man and First Woman created the white man and did they know what they were doing? Maybe a dark wind came up when they were being made, and it entered into the hearts of those new people.

The heap of blankets moves, and a hoarse voice comes out. "When the world was made, there was left-over material, all the bad parts of the weasel and the rattlesnake and darkness. And that is what —" he coughs and cannot continue. Aunt gives him juniper tea until he can go on.

"...what white people are made of," he finishes. Grandmother pats his feet under the blanket, but does not smile.

Kaibah looks at me with a question in her eyes, and I shake my head slightly. I know and she knows the true story, that the first white men came from the moon and will return there someday, leaving the earth to us.

Is Half-Alive Man getting better? Aunt hums softly to herself as she makes corn mush, and Grandmother's face looks brighter, calmer than I've seen before. But Half-Alive Man is like a shot deer that struggles to his feet one last time, only to fall back to the ground again.

The breathing terrifies us

All night long he breathes in a way I have never heard before. It sounds as if he cannot get enough air and is gasping for it. When that happens, Grandfather's arm stretches across his blanket, and Grandmother's hand clutches his. I imagine that a strip of sinew connects us all, and when Half-Alive Man stops breathing, everyone is pulled tight by that leather. Then when he sighs, we sigh with him, our hands unclench from the blankets, and the tight rope lets us go.

Kaibah whispers to me, "What will we do if he dies in the night? I am afraid!"

I am afraid, too, but I want to calm my sister. So I begin in a soft whisper, "If he dies during the night, the children of the ant people will come to carry him far away. We do not need to be afraid."

Sister wonders where they will take the body, and I answer, far, far away to a grove of tall pines beyond the canyon. Their feet will not be tired, their arms will not let the body drop, and we will all be safe. Finally, we fall asleep. But the next sound I hear is not his terrible breathing, but the wailing of my aunt that her husband is dead.

Evil comes two times this day

My mother used to say that when evil happens, it is never one thing, but more than one. And that is true this day, for soon after we leave the hogan and rub ashes on our faces to keep away the *chindi* — for we could not stay there with the body — we hear a warning shout from the lookout on the rim of the canyon. He has spotted soldiers at the mouth of the canyon!

Quickly, Grandmother rolls up the blankets and ties one to the back of each person in the family. To her son she gives a sack of dried pumpkins and peaches. To Grandfather she hands a sack with some bowls and pots, while she gives two water gourds to Kaibah and me. Poor Aunt is stumbling around in a daze, picking up one pot, then putting it down.

Grandfather turns at the door to tell us we are going to the house of the Ancient Ones, and the look on his face frightens me. Outside the wind blows sharp and clean, but there is no sunlight on the floor of the canyon, only a frozen river and drifts of snow. Aunt walks close to Grandmother, who keeps tugging on her hand to make her trot. I can see Starlight's head bobbing in the cradle board against her back. My other aunt asks what will happen to our sheep, but Grandfather says we cannot bring them with us; there is not enough time.

Our moccasins sink into the snow; luckily, Grandmother gave us leggings a few days ago, so our legs are protected. Holding tight to Sister's hand, I look around at my people hurrying beside the river. I touch the white shell necklace around my neck and pray for safety.

We climb the canyon wall

Soon, we reach the rock wall where the Ancient Ones built their house, halfway up. Grandfather and his son hurry forward, setting up a long, notched log against the canyon wall. It just reaches to the dark doorway above, and Grandfather is happy that he made it the right length.

Lightly, as quickly as a younger man, he puts one moccasined foot on the ladder, pulling himself up the tree trunk. Behind me, Kaibah grips my shoulder and whispers that she does not know if she can climb that — it is too high, too frightening.

"We have to!" I whisper back. Soon it is my turn — Grandmother has gone ahead, and I can see her feet kicking out as she climbs the last stretch into the doorway.

High Jumper helps me set one foot on the ladder. "I can do it!" I tell him fiercely, suddenly angry and not afraid. Though the ladder soars up above me, dark and threatening, I pretend it is a horse I am riding — a wild and untamed horse that I can master. So I come to the top of the ladder to find Grandfather holding out his arms to me, helping me swing through the doorway.

Kaibah is next; I do not cry out when I see her strained face against the wall, peering upward. Only, Grandfather reaches down so far it frightens me and hauls her up the last way.

Then comes Aunt, with her baby strapped to her back, then High Jumper, Partridge Girl, and her mother and father. We are all in a cold, gloomy room made of rock. A pale light comes in the two windows, but stays by the ledges. Little drifts of snow lie on the stone floor. I know we cannot make a fire to warm us, for that would alert the soldiers. We must just sit, wrapped in our blankets.

To keep the soldiers from finding us, Grandfather climbs back down again and hides the ladder behind some brush on the canyon floor. With a pine branch he sweeps away all of our footprints in the snow and climbs back up the cliff face, using small toeholds and handholds in the rock.

"There!" He swings through the door and sits, breathing loudly, on the cold floor. "There. Now let the sons of dung come and find us if they can!"

They come like a blue river

Cold, it is so cold in that still room. We hear sounds coming down the canyon — the clop of horses' hooves, shouts, cries, and something jingling. Grandfather sits by the side of the window, watching. He whispers to us that there are many soldiers below, a blue line as long as the river winding through the canyon. His voice is tired, and I know he thinks there are too many for us.

In the shadows of the room, I watch — our faces are all smudged from the ashes we smeared on after Half-Alive Man died. High Jumper's cheek twitches, and he drums his fingers against his leggings; Aunt sits slumped against the wall with her baby in her lap; Grandmother leans forward, straining to see through the window, while Uncle and my other aunt stand against the far wall, their faces lined and tense. We three girls huddle in a corner like wild grouse, not making a sound. I imagine the soldiers as fierce hawks diving down out of the sky.

They will catch us, maybe even kill us, and there is nothing we can do. *Oh, Changing Woman, hide us from the blue soldiers. Let them ride on through, seeing nothing.*

I feel like a sheep about to be killed

The soldiers camp below us, making fires and loud noises. From farther down the canyon we think we can hear other *Diné* shouting insults at the soldiers, but Grandfather will not let us make a sound. We cannot move until the soldiers go. The light by the window gets grayer and grayer, until finally it is black. When it is dark, Grandmother touches us silently, drawing us into the center of the room, where she hands around some dried cornmeal. I am too frightened to eat, though I hear munching and chewing sounds in the darkness.

Kaibah and I wrap up in our sheepskins, and the others make rustling sounds as they lie down on the hard, cold floor. I am grateful for our thick (and smelly) sheepskins. Pressing my nose into the wool, sniffing that safe, animal smell, I try to keep calm. But fear races inside my body like cold water; I cannot stop it, I can't be brave the way my mother wanted me to be.

The soldiers chop down our peach trees

The next morning, when the light is a cold gray, Grandfather kneels by the window. Suddenly his head snaps back, and he whispers, "They've captured our people and herded them together!" After a long moment, we hear a new sound outside, the dull thump of metal against wood. Again and again it comes, until something creaks and falls to the ground.

"*Chindi taa go,* curse them to no goodness!" Grandmother hisses, watching by the window. "They're chopping down our peach trees for their fires!"

Grandfather's hands tighten on his knees, until the cords in his fingers stand out. To me, he seems like a lean, old puma, lying on a branch. If he could, he would jump on those soldiers below and rake them with his claws. But the terrible thing is, High Jumper does it for him.

Without our seeing him, he has grabbed his father's weapons, knelt silently by the other window, and loosed an arrow.

"Foolish boy!" Grandfather dashes the bow to the ground, pulling High Jumper away from the window. But it is too late. Now they know where we are, and bullets *ping* off the rock wall. There are so many bullets being fired, it sounds like fat sizzling in a fire. All of us lie flat on the floor, hands over our heads. Aunt whimpers quietly nearby while her baby cries, but Aunt does not try to quiet Starlight, for it is no use now. I pull the sheepskins over my head and Kaibah's.

Then, after a terrible, noisy time, silence comes. Someone begins to speak outside. We raise our heads, daring to look up now that the bullets have stopped. Grandfather keeps frowning at High Jumper, but I smile at him — a small smile. For though he was foolish, he was also brave and did not want to be caught without fighting. I know how he feels.

The Nakai tells us to surrender

Words keep coming through the window, like birds darting into the room. At first, none of us can understand them, but my aunt, Mexican Woman, suddenly sits upright, listening. As the words continue, she stands and goes near the window, cupping her hand to one ear. It sounds like our language, but different.

Aunt tells us that the Mexican, the *Nakai*, is speaking Navajo — but badly. He says we must surrender, that there are too many soldiers for us to fight. He tells us the soldiers have rounded up more *Diné* from deeper in the canyon. Aunt makes a sour face. "He says they are our friends and will take us to their fort and feed us. They know we are starving."

The words stop for a moment, then go on. "Beef." I can understand that! I think because it is a Mexican speaking our language, the words sounded strange at first. "You will all have corn and other good things to eat," he says.

In the silence, High Jumper says that if the white men hadn't burned our fields, we wouldn't be starving now! The *Bilagáana* are lying to us, and we should never surrender.

But his father disagrees. Without food, how can we survive the long, cold time?

Kaibah whispers that beef would taste so good. I am too afraid to think about food. Silently, Grandfather looks around the room. He seems to be counting us, to be adding up something inside. Then he calls out the window that we will surrender, that we want no more fighting. When High Jumper makes a fierce face, Grandfather hushes him with a quick downward motion of his hand. "Gather your blankets, whatever you need to take with you. We are going with the soldiers," he says. "Better this journey than the road to starvation. Wife, I will climb down first to set up the ladder, then the rest of you follow."

High Jumper refuses to leave

One by one, we leave that cold, dark room and scramble down the ladder. When it is my turn, I peer out the window first. Below is a crowd of ragged *Diné* by the frozen river, with many mounted blue soldiers guarding them. Taking a deep breath, I back out the doorway and climb the notched tree trunk to the ground. Kaibah holds out her hand to me, and I take it. Only High Jumper does not join us.

Grandfather calls out to him, as does Grandmother and his mother and father. To each plea, he spits back that he would rather die here, in the *Dinetah,* that white men cannot be trusted, not ever. When one of the soldiers, a man with a red beard and a red face, raises his rifle, I yell, "No! Wait, wait!" Aunt shouts to the *Nakai* to tell the soldier not to shoot. The Mexican man is a small, wrinkled creature with skinny hair. I don't like his eyes or his pointy chin. But he speaks to the soldier with the strange red hair on his face, who lowers his rifle.

Grandmother calls that soldier *Hot Face* "because it looks like his face is on fire."

Then I shout up to High Jumper that he promised to protect me, that he is my friend, like a brother to me. It is all I can think of to persuade him. We wait for a moment, and his face appears at the window. Glancing down at me and back at the room, he slowly climbs out the doorway.

"Thank you, Sarah Nita." Grandmother grips my shoulder. "Thank you."

And when he is on the ground, he comes straight to me. In the middle of this terrible time, in the middle of the blue soldiers mounted on their huge, sweaty horses, my friend is beside me.

The long journey begins

Grandmother tells me that this is the worst part of her story. Once the blue soldiers captured them in the canyon and marched them off to Fort Defiance, then came the hardest time for all Diné. This was the beginning of the Long Walk.

I put some soft cloth in her lap so she can wipe her eyes from time to time. And there is a gourd of water beside her to refresh her lips. I am afraid of her getting too tired, but I think her anger gives her strength.

Mean Mouth shouts directions

There are so many men in blue! They make loud cries, their horses stamp, and all the time the *Nakai* is shouting directions to us. There are more of us Navajos than the white men, but they are stronger. They have horses, and guns.

First Hot Face shouts something that the *Nakai* then tells us. "Come in peace! We will take care of you and give you warm clothing and food."

Heads stir, as if a wind passed over a grove of trees. "Food, blankets, beef...," come the words. "We will come with you, we cannot live here anymore, we are starving," says one elder with a band of cloth wrapped around his head. Others repeat that they are starving.

The *Nakai* orders us to follow, wheeling his spotted horse around, heading for the canyon mouth. "Make a line, all together! You can bring your animals."

Kaibah names him Mean Mouth for his tight, skinny lips, and I pull hard on her hand, reminding her that he understands our language and that we must be careful.

Partridge Girl holds tightly to my left hand, pressing her head into my side.

Mean Mouth tells us that we are going to the Place of Soldiers, where we will be protected from our old enemies, the Utes. The white men will help us and feed us, for they can see that we are starving. Now is the time to stop raiding and stealing and become the kind of people that the Great White Father wants us to be.

I am so confused and afraid that the words stream over me like smoke. Where are they taking us? Will they kill us along the way?

We cannot find Silver Coat

Kaibah calls for our dog, but where is he? Has a soldier stolen him, or did he run away? When my sister darts out to search for Silver Coat, she does not listen to our calls. One soldier dismounts and runs after her, bringing her back to us. When I step forward, fists clenched, Grandfather grips my shoulder. But even I can see the soldier is not hurting Kaibah. Gently, almost, he hands her to us, saying some strange words that sound like *bkther, gurll.* His gray eyes shine like mica at the bottom of a river as he smiles at Sister, but I do not trust him. Mica Eyes, I name him silently.

Grabbing her arm, I give her a little shake — for frightening me — and a strange sound blasts through the air, making us all jump. The horses prance forward as the soldiers ride beside and in back of us to keep us moving. "When I look over my shoulder, the shuffling line of *Diné* makes me dizzy." My people's faces are weary, lined with cold and hunger. Dressed in torn blankets, some are almost naked and have only a few herd animals ahead of them.

When we pass our hogan, Grandmother asks permission from Mean Mouth to get her herd animals. At a nod, Grandfather and High Jumper open the brushwood corral and gather our goats and sheep. We have more animals than most, and I hear Grandfather saying we must guard them well, for they might be our food on the journey ahead.

Wet snow hits my cheeks as the canyon walls get lower; we are almost at its end. Grandfather casts a worried glance at the skies. Is he afraid, as I am? How will Kaibah survive this weather? And what of Grandmother, my two aunts, and Starlight? I am not so worried about the others.

There is only one good thing to take out of this wounded time, and Kaibah knows it, too. "Sarah Nita? Will we see our mother and father at the Place of Soldiers?"

I look down at her and say that I don't know, but we will look, and we won't stop looking until we find them.

Five hands of soldiers

When we reach the mouth of the canyon, there are more soldiers waiting there, with heavily loaded mules. I wonder if food is in those packs, and Grandmother says she hopes so. She is holding tight to Grandfather's hand, helping him move forward. In the time in the rock house he was fierce and protected us, but now that we are captured, his shoulders sag and his feet move slowly.

My sister walks beside me, shaking the snow out of her moccasins from time to time, for the snow comes well over our feet now. I promise that when we stop, I will stuff more dried grass into her moccasins to keep her warm. I have to take care of her; I cannot shuffle, or droop, or fall behind. Besides, the soldiers might do something terrible to me if I do!

Kaibah looks ahead of us and behind, then whispers, "There are five hands of soldiers, Sarah Nita."

I am afraid she is too tired to think, but she repeats, "Five hands of soldiers," explaining that if she counts on both hands to ten, then she has to do that five more times to count all the soldiers, and that there are even more of us.

Huddled in our blankets, we march up the hill, over the snowy land with the wind whistling past. The only sounds are old ones coughing, babies crying, and the bleating of the sheep.

Soldiers shout at us

They don't like it if we stop. Once we are on the high, brushy country overlooking the canyon, Slim Woman stops to use the bushes. Riding in from the side, a blue soldier shouts at her, holding up his rifle. Is he afraid she might run away? Frightened, she pulls her dress and blanket about her and runs to catch up.

"*Chindi taa go!*" Grandmother hisses, offended.

I, too, want to curse the soldiers.

Later, the wind grows stronger, blowing in our faces,

and our whole line slows down. I can hear people coughing behind me, and I see an old grandmother wrapped in a brown blanket stop in her tracks, leaning into the wind. A girl tries to urge her forward as a soldier rides up, shouting and waving his rifle.

"Chindi taa go!" Kaibah says this time.

Finally, the soldiers let us stop to rest, and we collapse on the ground, with the snow still falling. They hand out pieces of something white and hard that the *Nakai* tells us is *bread*. It does not taste very good, but it fills up my insides. Some of us are wondering where the beef is, but we are too afraid to ask. While we rest, I help Kaibah scrape away the snow and find grass underneath. Shaking it clean, I stuff it into her moccasins.

I use the bushes to relieve myself and hope none of the *Bilagáana* will shout at me. High Jumper stands with his back to me, glaring at the soldiers. He is keeping guard, and if a soldier decides to ride at me, he will jump out — like his name — to stop him.

Then that strange sound comes again, starting up the march, and we push through snowy grass and bushes toward the place of the rising sun. So far we are all keeping up with the soldiers. I am afraid of what will happen if we do not.

We get beef

Sometime toward the end of day, the snow stops. As the light goes, the blue soldiers dismount, hobble their horses, and start fires on the high plateau. Though I am shivering, first I look off in the distance to see if Silver Coat has followed us.

"Silver Coat?" I call. And Kaibah shouts, "Silver Coat? Come here!" There is no sign of him, and we are too busy to look, for Kaibah and I have to care for our animals, scraping away snow so they can eat the dried grass. None of us can find water nearby; there is only what we have brought with us in our gourds.

The pack mules did carry food, for a soldier brings out hunks of raw meat. The *Nakai* tells us to get in small groups and sit around a fire with a headman — which we do, putting Grandmother's rugs beneath us. Grandfather tries to tell the *Nakai* that we don't have headmen, but Mean Mouth declares that Grandfather will be in charge of us.

In our group, besides us, are two elders, and I recognize the old woman in a brown blanket who had trouble keeping up. There is a grim-faced man with a thin wife, two younger boys, and a girl about my size. The soldier hands my grandmother pieces of beef as big as one hand, which she cooks on sharp sticks over the fire.

After she offers a mouthful to the flames and says a prayer, Grandmother distributes the cooked beef. I tear into mine like a wolf. While we are eating, we tell each other our names and clans. The other grandmother is called Dezbah, and she is having trouble eating the meat, for most of her teeth are gone. The other grandfather says how delicious the food is, and how the white people cannot be all bad, for they are giving us such good meat.

Uncle thins his lips. *He* does not believe that! Then a delicious smell floats toward us, something I've never smelled before. The soldiers come around again with some metal cups — Grandfather has one to share with us. We all sip the hot black drink, and it warms my belly.

Kaibah's eyes widen. "Good!"

I feel I could march for days just on its smell. Mean Mouth says this drink is called *kaffi*.

"The soldiers can't be all bad, Sister, if they give us such good food." Kaibah leans tiredly against me, her head nodding.

We sleep outside in the snow

A soldier yells some words — I guess his command —
to other soldiers. Mean Mouth hurries around from
group to group like a young sheepdog, full of his own
importance.

"Lie down, all of you, for the night. Wrap up in your
blankets by the fire."

"Sleep out in the open?" Grandmother grumbles.
"Are these people human beings?"

Patting her arm, Grandfather says that if we bundle
ourselves up in all of our blankets and huddle close to the
fire, we will survive. But I worry about Starlight. The
soldiers have put up tents and have protection from the
fierce winds of the high country, but we have nothing!

Grandfather tells us where to sleep beside the fire and
to lie close to each other. Aunt and her baby are in the
middle; on one side of her are Uncle, my other aunt,
Slim Woman, and High Jumper; on the other side are
Partridge Girl, Kaibah, and me, with Grandmother and
Grandfather last. The rest of our group completes the
circle around the fire, huddled in blankets like us. I can
hear Dezbah coughing as we settle down.

I wish my grandmother would be in the middle,

where it is warmest, but she gives me a fierce look, point-ing her finger at the ground where I should lie. So we unroll our sheepskins from home and curl up by the fire. I put part of my sheepskin over Grandmother's bony legs and hug her tightly.

"My granddaughter," she says softly.

I am glad to be someone's granddaughter on this high land with the wind biting my cheeks and the stars like fierce white eyes above.

A cold nose at night

It is too cold to sleep, and I wish I had a roof over me. I remember how Coyote ruined the patterns of the stars in the sky, scattering the mica pieces here and there. If only someone were awake to tell me a story! When I turn over, bumping Kaibah and Grandmother, something chilly pokes my cheek. With a yelp, I jump up, ready to grab a burning stick from the fire.

But the creature bowing before me, grinning and wagging his tail, is not a wolf, it's Silver Coat! Now Kaibah is awake and she throws her arms around our dog, hugging him close. Grandmother grumbles sleepily that all the freezing air is getting under her blanket. So, carefully, we tuck the blankets around us, telling our dog to lie at our feet.

Kaibah whispers that he must have followed us from the canyon, maybe afraid of all the blue soldiers and the noise. But he's here, and tomorrow I'll worry about how to feed him. Now I can sleep, with my feet warm from his body, knowing that something from home is with Kaibah and me once more.

The goat is stupid

In the gray light of morning, I look around at the huddled shapes by the dying fire. Grandmother is already awake, rubbing her face and slapping her arms against her body. I am so stiff that I stumble when I get to my frozen feet, but if I step on them hard, the feeling comes back to them. Silver Coat bows to each member of our family in turn, and everyone remarks on what a brave, clever dog he is for finding us.

We are lucky that the soldiers let Grandmother bring her goats along. While others are eating the food from the soldiers, she milks the two goats, collecting the liquid in the metal pot she brought with her. Mixed with some ground corn, we have mush for breakfast, and it tastes so good. This is *our* food, not the white man's food. Only I wish for some of that kaffi they gave us last night.

At the sound of the *bugle* (that's what we learned it's called) we start out again, marching in a line with some soldiers ahead and some behind. I see Hot Face ahead, with his wild red hair sticking out from his hat, and nearby is the tall, lean form of the man I call Mica Eyes. They are the only ones I can tell apart, for these *Bila-gáana* all look alike to me with hair all over their faces, like wolves.

I herd the goats, using a knotted rope, while Kaibah and High Jumper keep the sheep together. But that bad goat, the black and white one, keeps stopping to graze, pawing at the snow and ripping up dried hunks of grass. After the fifth time I hit her, she bucks, gives me a mean look, and bounds away. As I chase after her, Silver Coat dashes ahead, but I stop at a soldier's shout. Does he think I'm running away? I drop to the ground and clap my hands over my ears as he shouts again. Horse's hooves pound past me as he races behind the goat and herds her back to us. He's helping me instead!

I run up and hit the goat's rump while Silver Coat nips her twice on each leg. Between us, we bring her back to Grandmother's side. Nodding to the soldier, I try to thank him, though I have no words he can under-stand. When Kaibah smiles at him, and he smiles back, I see that it is the thin soldier I call Mica Eyes.

"Pretty sister, don't smile at him! He could hurt us."

She looks puzzled, not understanding me. "But Sarah Nita, 'even among enemies, there can be a friend,'" she repeats one of Mother's sayings. I wonder and do not answer.

I make a friend

The girl in our group who eats with us comes up to me and asks if she can walk with me. When I nod, she tells me her name is Sah-nee, and that she has twelve sum-mers, just like me. She is a little smaller than I am, with thin wrists sticking out from her ragged, gray blanket. With uncombed hair hanging about her face, it is hard to see her eyes, but her voice is gentle and kind. The two other boys in our group are her younger brothers, and I have not heard them say a word. Maybe they are too frightened.

"I was afraid when I saw that soldier riding after you!" Sah-nee says.

I tell her that my insides felt like water, but Kaibah

reminds me that her soldier — now he is *her* soldier — is a nice person, not full of dark winds the way High Jumper thinks all white people are.

Sah-nee does not agree or disagree with my sister, but just asks if I noticed that our names start with the same sound. "Like the wind," she says. Then she wonders if I have made my first rug yet. I will not tell her how many times I had to rip out the wool and start over. So we talk of making rugs, the colors and patterns we like, and the songs we sing when weaving. She was using the cloud-ladder pattern in her rug, and so was I!

The right song is important, she says, to make the weaving right. *Song* echoes inside me, and I think of how words and music join us together, how they can heal a sick person, how they can make corn grow. Suddenly I wonder: Is there a song that will help us reach the end of our journey?

We reach the fort

On the fourth day of our journey we march over the flat land beside tall mountains. The wind is cruel here, seeming to gain speed as it spins off the mountains and whirls down on us. I don't know how Sah-nee's grandparents are surviving, but somehow they do. My grandparents help when they can, and High Jumper walks beside Dezbah, shouldering her weight, for she is having trouble keeping up.

Then the land narrows down as we enter a valley with low hills around it. "The Place of Soldiers . . . the fort," people call out excitedly. Maybe we will have a chance to rest and get warm!

Below are long buildings, like dark, old bones. Soldiers are marching and blowing on those foolish bugles. Horses stamp, and mules bray while all around on the low hills are so many of our people, they look like flocks of sparrows in the snow.

"More than I can count on my hands," Kaibah said. "Do you think . . . ?" She is afraid to say the words, and I am afraid to finish for her.

My heart beats faster, and under the sheepskin that is around my shoulders, I begin to sweat. What if our family isn't here?

Shouting and urging their horses on, the soldiers try to move us faster toward the fort. We gather enough strength to walk more quickly. Noise swirls around me like clouds: sheep bleating, dogs barking, babies crying, and families calling out greetings to our people who are already here.

The soldiers have to ride closer, to keep us together. Hot Face is shouting strange words at us: *"Siddown, siddown!"*

The *Nakai* tells us to sit on the hills so we can be counted. No one can understand why they would want to do this, and I can hardly wait until they are done. Finally, they are, and I ask Grandmother if I can go looking for my mother and father.

"Of course, my child, go look. May you find them." She has already sent High Jumper and Partridge Girl off to search for wood to make a fire, but I wonder if any wood is left with so many *Diné* camping here.

Holding hands, Sister and I go from group to group. "Have you seen Long Mustache, of the Bitter Water People?" Kaibah asks softly.

"And Glenbah, of the Salt People?" We are gripping hands so tightly that our nails are digging into our palms. But people shake their heads, smiling sadly. One man reminds me that many of us have lost relatives, but I don't want to hear his words, and walk swiftly on.

Again and again we ask, looking into people's faces, waiting to hear the words we yearn to hear. All afternoon we climb up and down the hills, threading through the crowds camped outside the fort. Some have made blanket tents that lean into the wind; one shelter has a fresh cowhide for a roof. Another family managed to dig out a small hole in the slant of a hill. But no one has seen our family, no one has heard of them. One woman tells us that the soldiers took an earlier group of Navajos to another fort, "a place far away by a river," she adds, "a place called the Bosque Redondo. Maybe your family was in that other group."

Kaibah presses her head against my arm, mouthing those strange words, but I am so sad, I can hardly comfort her. When I return, Grandmother looks up with a small smile, but it dies when she sees my face.

"Come, then." She holds out her arms. "Get warm by the fire."

High Jumper spreads a blanket for us to sit on, Silver Coat sits on my foot, and everyone gives us small pats and nods. But all I can see is water dropping from my eyes onto the gray and brown blanket, making little pools, and I wonder if my family is even alive.

They give us a strange white food

That night the soldiers bring around our portion of beef, enough for the sixteen of us. Sah-nee bites off small bits, feeding Dezbah, who is slumped, coughing, by the fire. Our grandmother has given Dezbah one of our blankets, but I don't know if it is helping.

The soldier gives us some white powder in a metal container and makes some motions with his hands, saying a word that sounds like a horse sneezing: *"Flaarhh!"*

"What is he saying?" Aunt wonders. We are having trouble hearing as Starlight cries and wails at Aunt's breast. Maybe the baby can't get enough milk.

"I don't know what to do with this food," Grandmother complains. "Should we cook it, like our cornmeal, or eat it the way it is?" Dipping my hands into it, I lick it off my fingers. It makes me cough, it is so dry and dusty. We wonder if it is some kind of earth the white men dug up, or something from a tree.

Aunt tells me to add some water from her gourd, and I stir the white dust into a paste. Put it on the fire, Grandmother says, and I set it over the coals. Kaibah looks around and tells us that other people are doing the same thing, cooking up the white dust in metal containers or eating it plain from their hands.

"How do you know when it is cooked?" Slim Woman wonders. "Maybe we need to add some wood ashes." She tosses in a handful of juniper ash, the way we would when cooking corn mush. When I peer in, the flaarhh does not look cooked — it is a soupy mush. But food must not be wasted, so we all have some to eat, though Grandfather spits it out and wipes his mouth against his sleeve, and Uncle frowns as he chews.

Aunt seems to like it best and finishes what we cannot. "I think we had this back when I was little, but I don't remember very well," she says.

If Kaibah and I are going to survive, to find our mother and father again, we must eat — even if we hate the food.

Uncle makes us tents

That night, after eating our food, Uncle decides that we must not sleep out in the open anymore. Now that we are staying in one place, we can make some kind of shelter. He sends the four of us children off to gather long poles, but it takes us almost until darkness to find them. There is not much wood left nearby, and we have to travel over the hills to collect some long sticks.

When we come back, Grandfather and Uncle have already made eight holes in the earth, holding burning sticks to the soil to unfreeze it. Singing a song of house building, Uncle forces the poles deep into the ground, then beckons Grandmother to bring her blankets. We are lucky that she has extra ones with her, unlike some of our people who seem to have none.

Grandmother and my two aunts drape the blankets over the poles, stitching them in place with some threaded sinew. As the sun sets, the red light falls on our two shelters. Tonight we will be warm!

My aunt is sick

For the first time in days, we sleep as soon as our heads touch the rugs beneath. Now the stars cannot look down on me like fierce eyes; now the wind is *outside*. But sometime in the night I feel a cold breeze when the blanket is pushed open. Someone is being sick, the harsh sounds coming through the blankets. When I crawl out into the night, afraid it is Grandmother, Aunt is clutching her stomach and moaning. "That *Bilagáana* food. It is bad for our stomachs!"

I get her some water and help her back to her place inside our tent. Starlight is fast asleep, curled under the gray blanket. If she is to live and survive, we must make sure that Aunt has enough to eat; otherwise, her milk will dry up, and Starlight will have nothing to eat.

There *must* be a way to cook this new food. I will watch tomorrow and see if the soldiers eat it, and if they do, *how* they do it.

Kaibah and I learn about flaarhh

Aunt is having trouble nursing Starlight again, as the baby wails and kicks her feet. Grandmother thinks that it is because Aunt is not getting enough food. You have to have a full belly to make milk for your baby, says Grandmother in a bitter voice, fanning the fire with the end of her blanket.

Before Sah-nee is awake and her family unwrapped from their coverings, Kaibah and I walk through the camp, looking at people around their fires. How are they cooking this new food? I see one woman stirring the dust in a metal pot, making a sour mouth.

"It tastes terrible, doesn't it?" I ask, and she agrees. Kaibah thinks we are cooking it the wrong way, and the woman nods. But how?

Down through the camp we wander, watching, looking, but no one seems to know how to prepare this food, and others have been sick during the night. One man wonders if the white men are trying to poison us.

Hurrying, Kaibah and I go down to one of the buildings of the fort. I know that my mother would hate to see me trying to learn from the *Bilagáana,* but she is not here. Pulling her hair around her face, as if it could hide her, Kaibah steps more and more slowly. Quietly, carefully as deer moving through shadows, we stalk one of the buildings. Bodies of animals are hanging from the roof of the building, a terrible smell coming through the door. We hurry on to another building, where men in blue are stirring things in big pots on huge metal boxes.

"Like giants, Sister!" Kaibah whispers to me. Then I hear one of them laugh as he sees us hiding near the doorway. We try to dart away, but he runs after us and grabs Kaibah's hand. When I look, it seems I am looking up, and up and up, he is so tall. Then I see his lean face — he only has hair under his nose — and his gray glittering eyes. It is Kaibah's soldier!

I tug on her other hand, but he will not let her go. My little sister is braver than me, for she opens her mouth and asks, "Flaarhh?"

He takes us inside the building and points to a soldier who is mixing the white dust with water in a big wooden bowl, punching it down and rolling it over. Mica Eyes pulls off a piece and offers it to Kaibah, who grimaces and waves her hand, "No."

Laughing, her soldier flattens the food with his hand and tosses it into a pan to cook on the huge metal box. He turns it over, blows on it to cool it, and offers it again to us. Sister holds it up to her nose, smells it, and takes a tiny bite. This time Kaibah smiles.

"Try it, Sarah Nita. It is good!"

I hold it to my nose and breathe in; it does not smell like our food, of the forests, the earth, the animals. Like Silver Coat nipping at a snake, I dart at it and take a quick bite. How could Kaibah think this is good? But it is food, and now that we know what to do, we both smile, nod, and turn away from Mica Eyes.

Giving Kaibah a little push with his hand, he says a funny word: *Scootnugh!*

"Scootnugh!" we say to each other, smiling. "Scootnugh!" running up the hill.

The story of Scootnugh

That word with its funny sounds makes my head whirl. Other words come darting in like little foxes trying to squeeze inside a den all at once.

"Scootnugh was a little fox," I tell Sister, who slows at the top of the hill. "She lived with her three brothers and two sisters in a nice sandy den at the foot of a juniper."

We sit down near one family as I tell the story.

"But Scootnugh wished to be something else. She did not want fur that had to be licked. She hated her bushy tail that got caught in the cracks of tree trunks. She wanted to be a goose — with a long, beautiful neck, who sailed on a shining river.

"One night she went to see a medicine man, asking if he had any medicine to change her form. He told her that only bad people wanted to change their shapes, and to go away.

"Dragging her tail, Scootnugh went back to her den. She played with her brothers and sisters, but not as much as before. When Father brought meat for her, she would hardly nibble it. She grew thinner and thinner, until she looked like a wisp of gray smoke. And no pleadings of her mother and father could get her to eat.

"On a night of the full moon, she wobbled out of the den. Not far away was a water hole that held a shimmer of white water. Staring at it, Scootnugh went forward, wishing as hard as she could to be a goose.

"One step, two, her paws left the dry ground and rested in the cool water. As she dropped her body under the water, her head sank onto her breast, which was suddenly round and smooth. With a quick shake, her tail disappeared and became long, gray feathers.

"When she opened her beak to thank the gods, a wild sound flew out. Beating her wings, she rose up, up from the water into the night sky. She seemed to be riding on moonlight, cool under her body.

"Again she cried her wild call — 'Free, free!'"

I pause for a moment, the words swirling in my head.

"And that is the way we will be one day. Like that goose, free in our land again."

Kaibah leans against me as people call out and sigh. An elder weeps, pressing her sleeve to her eyes, repeating the word, *free.*

Like the call of a wild goose, the word flies around me, off into the gray sky.

Kaibah and I cook flaarhh

When we reach our group, Kaibah tells me that my stories make her strong, that they make her legs move over the ground. They make my bones strong, too, and I wonder if this gift of telling stories is part of the inside wind that my uncle told me about.

At the end of the day, Kaibah and I plan our big surprise. We are all sitting in a group, the way the soldiers order us to, waiting for our portion of beef. Dezbah is sitting straighter tonight, looking stronger. I think she did not eat the strange white food, so she did not get sick. Sah-nee's father still looks hard and angry, and I have hardly heard him say two words. Maybe I should tell him the story about Worried Girl, and how she changed into the Girl Who Chased Away Sorrow.

When the soldier gives Grandfather a big, thick hunk of meat, we can hardly wait. Sah-nee's two brothers lean forward and touch the beef, licking their fingers. Sharply, Grandmother tells them to wait, that Grandfather must say a prayer first.

After we gulp down our meat (saving some for Silver Coat) Kaibah and I mix a little water with the flaarhh, stirring it in the metal pot. I ask High Jumper to pull two flat rocks onto the coals, and Sister and I press some of the dough onto the rocks to cook. We turn it over, waiting until both sides are brown, then break it into pieces and offer it around.

"Mmmm." Grandmother sighs. "This is better, not as dusty."

At first Aunt is afraid to eat, but we tell her it will not make her sick cooked this way, that even the soldiers eat it.

"You need the food for Starlight," Kaibah says in a grown-up voice. Gently, she rubs the baby's cheek and sings a little song to her.

High Jumper smiles at me when I hand him his food, and I feel warm inside that I can help his family. They have given so much to Kaibah and me that I am happy to give something back.

I cannot be patient

I ask Grandfather when we will leave for the fort by the river as I step from foot to foot, hating the way my dirty woolen dress scratches my skin above the leggings.

He rests a hand on my head. "I do not know the soldiers' plans for us, Sarah Nita. We will have to be patient. I have seen them getting wagons ready, putting things in the back under those white covers. Maybe soon."

Patient! Didn't my mother say I was like a little goat that had to be pulled by a rope? Didn't she always wonder how my hair got like tangled yarn, asking why I forgot to wash my face with snow in the winter?

I did try to remember. I saw my two aunts scooping up snow to rub on their faces. Even Kaibah remembers to rub snow on her face, tries to run her fingers through her hair. Is that why Mica Eyes likes her? Because she is almost clean and has a gentle face? I know I do not look gentle; I look stormy and angry, but I think that that is how I will survive the Time of Soldiers.

High Jumper is restless, too

High Jumper comes up to me, brushing his hair back from his forehead. He is sooty and unwashed, like all the rest of us, and tries to keep clean by scrubbing his face with snow, but it just streaks the dirt. He says that he cannot be patient, either, and that he has been talking to some other boys who are planning to run away one night soon.

I look around quickly. No one seems to hear. Grandmother tells us to find some wood for the fire, or if we can't find wood, to gather some dried dung. Together, we walk down to the camp buildings, searching the ground for fuel. But everyone else is doing the same thing! We look like birds pecking in a cornfield, heads bobbing up and down.

"You would not run away, would you?" I ask quietly as High Jumper seizes a piece of wood near a building.

"I don't know." He tells me he hates living all pushed together with so many of our people, and that he doesn't trust the blue soldiers, even though they are feeding us. There is nothing to do except wait. Yet he doesn't want to leave his grandfather and grandmother.

His foot taps the ground, and I think of a horse about to bolt. How can I persuade him to stay? The thought of him running off through the snow with no food frightens me, but all I can say is, "It would be dangerous, High Jumper. What if the soldiers chase after you or shoot you?"

He does not answer, and we return to camp with two pieces of wood and one bit of dried dung.

The soldiers get ready to leave

Before the sun rises on this windy, gray day, Sah-nee and I meet while gathering wood. We tell each other how our people are; my aunt's milk is still not very good, but my grandparents are not weak, not yet. Sah-nee tells me that Dezbah is so thin, she can see her bones poking out at the wrists, and it frightens her. And when her father talks, he uses words like, *betrayal . . . can't trust them.* He has relatives near Black Mesa, but Sah-nee's mother is trying to persuade him to stay.

As we head back to our camp, we notice soldiers hurrying about the fort in the dim light. They are hitching up wagons with white covers, putting things into them, holding their heads low against the cold wind.

Once the sun is up, some men in blue come around, the way they did when we first came to the fort. Grandfather says they are counting us; no one knows why. The soldier with the flaming red hair and fiery skin — Hot Face — marches past, calling out words we do not understand.

After him comes the *Nakai,* who tells us what the soldiers want. "Roll up your blankets, gather your animals. We leave today."

Kaibah, Partridge Girl, and I take down the blankets around our poles. The ones we won't wear on the journey our aunts tie tightly into bundles. High Jumper binds the long sticks together while Grandmother packs her pots and bowls into a leather sack. Grandfather and Uncle are herding the sheep and goats together, with Silver Coat helping.

While we work, High Jumper mutters, "At last we are moving! Any place will be better than this!"

But, I wonder, what if it's worse?

They herd us like sheep

Aunt shreds up the last of the cliffrose bark we could find, stuffing it under Starlight's bottom. Soon, the baby is wrapped and in her cradle board, and High Jumper lifts her onto Aunt's back, settling the blanket around Aunt's shoulders. He offers to carry Starlight when Aunt gets tired, and she gives him a gentle smile.

That strange, yelping sound comes from the bugle, and our people start moving like a river down the low hills, along the plain. Behind me, Sah-nee and her mother help support Dezbah while her two brothers dart in and out of the line. Her father is silent as always, with a fierce look on his face.

Kaibah puts her hands over her ears at the sound of horses stamping and whinnying, soldiers shouting, our people coughing, and babies crying until their mothers put them in their cradle boards and tuck them under blankets and shawls — if they have them.

As a gritty snow starts falling, we duck our heads and set our feet toward the place of the rising sun.

"It feels like freezing dust!" Kaibah says between her teeth. "I hope this does not keep up all the way."

I look at her; her cheeks are a little fuller now, after our time at the fort, and she doesn't look quite so thin. But I still worry about how she will make this long journey ahead of us.

Whistling to our dog, I grip Kaibah's hand in my left and Partridge Girl's in my right and am glad of the sheepskin over my back. *Oh, my mother, my father, will you be there to greet us?*

Will I ever sit next to my father again as he pretends to be a squirrel scampering up my arm, searching for nuts in my hair?

Who needs to be civilized?

As we march over the snow, Grandfather turns to look over his shoulder. "How will the old ones journey in this weather?" He seems to forget that he is old, too.

The *Nakai* comes riding up on his spotted horse, snow spurting from the hooves. He calls out, "Look how many of your people we've captured. We will civilize you, teach you to farm — all of you!" He sweeps his arm wide, then gallops off to join the soldiers.

"Civilize!" Grandfather mutters. He tells the behind of that horse that the *Diné* were here long before white people; that we know how to care for the earth, the forests, the animals, and the sweet water. It is the white man who needs to be civilized, he exclaims.

Sah-nee's father waves one arm angrily, saying, "We should teach *them!*" and others call out, agreeing with him.

I wish evil on the white men

Father always said that we must live in harmony with our world — with the red buttes, the mesas, sagebrush, male and female rains, snow in winter, antelope, deer, the wild turkey, and our people. "That is the Navajo way," he would tell me, his face solemn to show that this was important.

I have a small talk with my father inside as we march through the snow, cold seeping through the soles of my moccasins. *How can I be in harmony with white people? How can I be in harmony when my stomach feels sick from their food and my face is freezing?*

But there is no answer. I cannot even see my father's face inside, though it has only been a little over three moons since my family was captured. Father always told me I must never wish for evil to come on anyone. I knew — he knew — that he meant witches or skin-walkers; no one wanted to say that terrible word. But I am so angry now that I want to call down evil on these blue soldiers for what they are doing to us. In a small, hard voice I wish: *Let them all die of a horrible sickness. Let their teeth fall out and their insides turn to black water.*

But somehow those dark thoughts make me feel sick inside, as if I had eaten uncooked flaarhh. It does not make me feel happy to think of those soldiers slipping off their horses and dying on the way. If I were a singer, like my grandfather who died two summers ago, I would make up a song, a prayer to bring our family together.

Let us walk our earth again,
Let us be in the shadow of our hogan,
Let us sit by the fire, together.

Then I feel peaceful, not full of dark thoughts blowing like a fierce and terrible wind.

Will they make slaves of us?

What will happen to us when we get to this fort by the river? What if the *Nakai* is lying to us? Maybe they will make slaves of us there. Aunt talks to me on the march about what it is like to be a slave — she is worried, too. She remembers little of being a slave to the New Mexicans, but her mother told her you always have to do what someone else tells you. You must prepare your master's food, she says, and make beds, sweep houses, fetch water, chop wood, water their horses, and take care of their babies.

Thrusting out ten fingers, Aunt says, "I could fill each of these with something the master tells you to do! And they make up more things if they see you stopping!"

Everyone in our group has heard her, and our words buzz back and forth like angry bees. High Jumper comes close for a moment, saying that *he* will never be slave to a white man. He will run away first!

Grandfather hears and asks how his grandson will survive on his own, what will he eat? High Jumper slows to match his stride with Grandfather. "We *Diné* can always find food."

Sah-nee plucks my right sleeve and asks shyly if I think we will be slaves at the fort. I shake my head; who can know the minds of the *Bilagáana?*

The Nakai does not help us

We march all day through the falling snow, only resting for a short time to let our animals drink from a stream and eat some dried grass. After chewing on hard bread and drinking some water, we wrap ourselves tightly in our blankets and go on.

Soon the wind blows harder, colder, and Grandmother pulls the blanket around her face. Grandfather walks in front of Aunt to shield her and Starlight. I can hear the baby whimpering. Slower, slower we go as the snow comes down harder. Kaibah does not say one word, but she is biting her lip so hard, the blood comes.

Sah-nee's grandmother and grandfather are falling behind, feet barely moving. My friend is trying to help, but Dezbah slips to the ground like a heap of rags. Suddenly, Aunt marches forward to where the *Nakai* rides his spotted horse. I see her speaking to him; I see him waving his hand downward.

When Aunt returns, she's so angry, her cheeks glitter with tears. "They can do nothing for the old ones, he said. Either they keep up, or they will be left to die."

"Chindi taa go," Grandmother and Grandfather say together.

And so it is my elders who support Sah-nee's grandmother, helping her step by step until the light goes and we can huddle by fires to get warm. What will happen to her? What if she isn't strong enough to go on tomorrow?

We keep Dezbah warm

That night Grandfather brings Dezbah into our blanket shelter, putting her between me and Kaibah. "Keep her warm, my granddaughters," he says, spreading a blanket over us. We are crowded together — Grandfather, Grandmother, Aunt, and Starlight, and Kaibah and me with our dog on our feet. Between us Dezbah's body feels like bird bones — thin and brittle. I do not think that our warmth will be enough.

Kaibah asks for a story

The next day the snow stops, and a pale sun shines. This morning Sah-nee walks beside me, with Sister on my right. High Jumper is helping Dezbah to walk, holding one arm while my grandfather holds the other. Dezbah does not talk; her thin face looks pale and weary. I wish that we had enough blankets for all of them; it isn't fair that Sah-nee has to sleep out in the open with just one blanket for cover! But we do not have extras to share, and there is not enough room in our small shelters for her family, too.

Kaibah tugs on my hand, reminding me of the time I told a story to cheer up Father, to change his downward-turned mouth. "Remember? You called yourself The Girl Who Chased Away Sorrow."

Sah-nee asks about that story, but I shake my head. I cannot tell it today; it will make me too sad to remember when we all lived together in my mother's hogan with the warm fire burning and mutton stew bubbling in

the pot. Instead of warmth and good smells, I am surrounded by the sounds of shuffling feet, crying babies,
and coughing. Soldiers keep close watch on us, riding up
and down our line as the wagons follow at the rear. I
hope there is plenty of food in them.

"If you tell us a story, Sister," pleads Kaibah, "it will
help us to forget the cold, the soldiers, and this marching,
marching, marching."

The words float up

I don't answer right away. If I am quiet, out of the silence
words sometimes rise up like sparks from a fire. "Once,"
I begin, waiting for the words. Kaibah gives a little hop
beside me. "Once there was a family of prairie dogs who
lived in the sandy soil." More words come from inside,
and pictures, too. I am imagining how we all lived together in our hogan, and how we were like prairie dogs
in their safe burrow.

"They had everything they wanted — sunlight in the
morning, moonlight at night, sweet grasses outside their
burrow, a mother and father, and five brothers and
sisters to play with. Every day Smallest One poked her
head above the entrance and looked about. 'Any hawks?'

111

she asked herself, eyeing the blue sky. 'Any coyotes to crunch me in their teeth?' she asked. 'Any sharp-fanged rattlesnakes to eat me up?'"

Just ahead of us, Grandmother looks over her shoulder and smiles at me.

"Of course, after Smallest One asked herself all those questions, she darted back into her burrow. The world was too frightening, too scary. Her brothers and sisters teased her. 'Smallest One is a baby, a baby, she's afraid of her own shadow!'

"Every day the smallest prairie dog declared that *this* day she would be brave and finally leave the burrow. But she did not leave the safe dark of their home. The sun shone, birds flew, the moon shed its light over the red land, and she missed it all."

As I talked, the cold, snowy land fell away; the sounds of our people and the mounted soldiers disappeared.

"The others told her about the golden ball that rolled from one part of the sky to the other each day. She only saw shadows in the burrow. The others told her about the green leaves fluttering in the wind, and the cactus with beautiful yellow blooms. She only heard the sound of grasses rustling.

"And so it would have gone on forever, except that

one day clouds covered the sky, thunder boomed, and the rain began to fall. It ran down the tunnels, collected at the bottom, and water began to rise inside the burrow. 'Out, out, everyone out!' shouted Smallest One's father. Everyone raced for the entrance, popping out into the strong rain — all except the littlest prairie dog.

"But water rushed into the tunnels, there was less and less air to breathe, and soon Smallest One had to decide: Would she drown in their burrow or leave it for the outside world? She took a deep breath, said a prayer to the Holy People to protect her, and clawed her way to the entrance. As the rain stung her eyes, thunder boomed overhead. She almost ducked back inside, except the rising water was soaking her tail by now. So with one big leap she jumped out of the burrow and looked around. Where were her brothers and sisters? Where were her mother and father? She looked and looked but could see nothing in the driving rain and darkness.

"Nearby was a thorny shape with golden blooms that glowed when the lightning flashed. It looked safe to Smallest One, and she ran for it. The rain soaked her fur, right to her skin. Shivering, she ducked into the shelter of the cactus and was surprised to hear voices. 'Here she is, she's safe, she's safe!' came the voices of her family.

How happy she was to see them. How happy they were to see her!

"She was safe, but more than that, she had learned to leave her burrow. And when the rain stopped and the water sank into the dry ground, she stayed outside, nibbling on the grasses and drinking from the puddles.

"She always was the first to dive for the burrow at the cry of a hawk. She always was the first to hide when they heard a coyote howl. Still, every day she crept outside to eat, to watch the great sun roll overhead, and to smell the sweet air after a rain."

I look up to see that I am surrounded by people, not just Sah-nee, Sister, Partridge Girl, Grandfather, and Grandmother and their family, but many others.

"Thank you for the story!" they call out. And just then the soldiers blow their horns to stop the march so we can eat hard bread and drink water. As we slow down, High Jumper smiles at me, the scowl gone from his face. Today I chased away sorrow, for a time.

My terrible dream

At night I dream I am standing at the door to our hogan with my arms out. A black wind blows, bringing rain and lightning. I am screaming something into the wind, but no one hears. A body flies by in the wind, all its white bones shining. I wake myself up screaming, and everyone else is awake, too, asking what is wrong.

It is time to get up, to make a fire, to try to get warm for another day of marching. But I start the walk this day with a terrible heaviness in my chest.

The first death

At least it is not snowing when we pack up our blankets, gather our animals together, and set off — once again. But the cold seeps under our blankets, through the soles of our moccasins, and I see Grandmother stumbling once or twice over clumps of dried grass. High Jumper hurries to help her, and that leaves Sah-nee and her father trying to help Dezbah move forward.

Soon, they fall behind, and though we try to help them along, we are too heavily loaded. The last time I see them, they are two people standing still with a crumpled, dark shape between them. One person bends over, straightens, and moves forward again. I hear my friend's mourning wail on the wind.

No soldier stops to help. When Sah-nee joins us, she

speaks through her tears. "She is dead — all of a sudden. We had to leave her."

I hate that my dream came true, and I hate that Dezbah will not sleep beside me tonight.

This is the first death, and Grandfather says there will be many more.

Others slip away

Dezbah is not the only one to die this day. I see two elders stumbling and falling behind; a boy with a terrible cough collapses on the ground. I am afraid to look at them, but I have to count them — I have to remember. The soldiers shove their rifles at the relatives waiting by their dead ones, and our people must keep moving.

People are muttering around me, "They are not even human beings."

At night, when we camp, we put ashes on our cheeks for the dead, and I comfort Sah-nee. But it doesn't feel like a time of mourning; it feels like a time of anger. Some young men are clustered together around one fire, talking among themselves. Excitedly, High Jumper comes back to our fire, and crouches beside me. "Those men and some boys are going to run away tonight, Sarah Nita."

I ask if he's going; he doesn't say yes or no, but I can feel his restlessness like a sharp smell on the wind. When he enters his family's blanket tent soon after, I almost go up to Uncle to say, "Your son might run away. Talk to him!" But I can't tell my friend's secret. So I lie down silently, pulling the sheepskin up to my chin. When I wake in the morning, will he be gone?

Sah-nee comes with us

In the morning, Sah-nee pushes aside our blanket door and cries, "They're gone, Sarah Nita! My father and brothers ran away with the others!"

Holding my friend's hand, I run to Uncle's tent to see if High Jumper is still there. He is outside by their fire, feeding it dry sticks. "So you stayed," I whisper to him, and he smiles quickly, telling me he was afraid to leave his grandparents.

Wrapping a gray blanket tightly around himself, Grandfather goes to talk with some other men to find out what's happened. Grandmother cooks flat bread for us over Uncle's fire. She is always careful to save some of our food from the night before, not like some families who eat all their food at once.

When Sah-nee collapses by the fire, Grandmother touches her shoulder. "You must share our blanket tent at night; bring your mother and grandfather, too. Somehow we will make room."

The first thing that my aunt, Mexican Woman, does, is make Sah-nee sit on the rug in our tent. Taking out her stiff grass brush, she brushes my friend's hair until tears come to Sah-nee's eyes. Aunt gives her a length of red wool to bind around her hair.

"Even though we are captives, we are still 'the People,'" Aunt says firmly. "We must stay clean, keep our faces washed, pray to the Holy People, and keep living the way we were meant to."

Sah-nee nods at Aunt's words. All day she walks with us, helping with the animals and gathering firewood at night. I am sad for her but glad that now I have another sister!

We find the monster's blood

We march for days and days, through snow, over snow, sometimes finding water, sometimes not. We reach the country where we walk between tall red buttes speckled with green junipers, where the wind howls at our backs. One day Grandfather takes a stick and pokes through the snow, scattering it.

"I thought it was here! This is where Monster-Slayer killed the evil giant; there's its dried blood on the ground." We all come to look, kneeling by Grandfather and poking fingers through the snow. Hard black mounds cover the soil, and we draw our fingers back quickly. This is something from the Long Ago Time, to be spoken about but not touched.

But all day our moccasins hit the hard, uneven rock beneath, and by nighttime Kaibah is limping badly. She tells me she twisted her ankle on "it," refusing to use the words *monster's blood*.

Grandmother steeps some herbs in hot water that night, soaking a rag in it and wrapping it around Sister's ankle. It seems to help, and Kaibah finally sleeps beside me, with Sah-nee at my back. Silver Coat curls on our feet, helping to keep us warm. My friend's grandfather and mother are wedged beside Grandmother. But I lie awake for a time, listening to the soldiers marching around camp, listening to their strange, harsh words that sound like pebbles hitting a bowl. How will my sister walk tomorrow?

Mica Eyes helps

All morning Kaibah limps beside me; I hold one arm while High Jumper holds the other. But we are falling behind, and I am afraid; I think that death waits at the end of the line. Trying to hurry, biting her lip, Kaibah says, "I can't keep up. It hurts too much," and she sits down in the snow.

"No, Sister! You can't fall behind, you can't!" Then High Jumper puts her on his back and goes forward, a step at a time. But he is tired, too, his mouth tight with the effort of holding Kaibah.

A horse's hooves pound beside me. I crouch, terrified, as the horse comes to a stop. Mica Eyes swings down from his mount, kneeling beside Kaibah. She points to her ankle, showing him how red and swollen it is under the bandage.

Making a clicking sound with his teeth, he gently lifts

Kaibah onto his horse. As High Jumper steps forward, he waves his hand at him and smiles.

"No hrrrt, no hrrrt," he tells us, but the *Nakai* is not here to help us understand. Besides, what can the two of us do against a mounted soldier?

On top of the horse, Kaibah calls out that she will be all right. The soldier swings up behind her, putting one arm around her middle and using the other to hold the reins. They ride away from us.

High Jumper is puzzled and confused. Is that soldier just being kind? How could that be?

Kaibah rides with Mica Eyes

There is no snow today! I can lift my face to the sharp blue sky and feel no gritty flakes. Grandmother and my two aunts bless the sun for its warmth, and Aunt takes the blanket away from Starlight's face to give her fresh air and sunshine.

As we roll up our blankets and tent poles, Mica Eyes leads his horse over to us, signaling to Kaibah to mount. "Cmmm, grrll," he says, and she knows what he means! Looking over her shoulder and smiling, Kaibah tells us that her soldier taught her some words on the journey yesterday. That strange sound, *cmmm,* means he wants her to ride with him. And *grrll* is their word for a *Diné* granddaughter.

Grandfather frowns at Grandmother but says nothing. I clench my fists; now Sister is learning *their* words and is riding with one of *them.* Kaibah is the only one in our family who looks happy as she holds out a hand to her soldier. Quickly, she swings up, her limp right foot dangling against the horse's side. Then Mica Eyes does something strange: He touches one finger to his hat before urging his horse on. What does that mean?

For the rest of the day, my sister is with Mica Eyes, only joining us for food and at nighttime, when Grandmother soaks a new bandage in herbs and wraps it around Sister's ankle. I am afraid of what she is learning, afraid that that blue soldier will take her away from us.

The robbers come

After another day of riding with Mica Eyes, Grandmother declares that my sister is better, and she can walk with us again. Sister does not dare disobey her and sets off with Sah-nee, Partridge Girl, and me. We walk a little slower than usual, so Kaibah will not get too tired.

Partridge Girl is happy to have her friend back and asks if Sister will play the string game with her that night. As they are talking, I hear sounds behind — cries and shouting. Hooves thud on the hard earth as men on horseback gallop up to our line.

"Hide!" Aunt cries. "Hide!"

Throwing ourselves to the ground, we pull our blankets over our heads. Hooves thunder close by, and I have to look. One man races up to us so close, I can see his black mustache blowing and his thick black eyebrows. Holding out one arm, he snatches up a little girl nearby. She cries out, but no soldier goes to help her. Our people try to stop the horse, but he thunders ahead. Another man cuts through our line, grabbing a young boy and throwing him across his horse as a third man on horseback drives a group of sheep and goats away from the line. Grandmother shouts, "My goats!"

Running after the raider, someone is taking great, leaping strides, whirling his rope around his head. He is shouting something at them, a terrible word. It is High Jumper, trying to save our animals! But no matter how fast he leaps and runs, he cannot keep up with the men on horseback. Finally, he stops, turns, and walks back to us with dragging feet. The raiders gallop away, with their captured animals ahead of them and some children thrown across the necks of their horses.

Aunt places one hand on all of us, as if she is counting and making us safe. Grandmother breathes out a prayer, and Uncle stares off at the disappearing animals. "Probably New Mexicans," he tells us, "getting rich from our sorrow. They will sell the children as slaves."

Beside me, Sah-nee is trembling, holding on to my arm. But Kaibah and I are not crying. The soldiers do not care if our animals are stolen; they do not care if *we* are stolen. No one goes after the thieves, no soldier tries to recapture our animals or rescue the children.

I smile a special smile at High Jumper, proud that he tried to save our goats. "You ran fast, but the horses were faster."

He does not smile back but just hits his leg with the knotted rope. It almost seems he is trying to hurt himself.

He disappears

All night Kaibah and I sleep with our arms around each other, and in my dreams, I see that man with the dark mustache swooping up the girl onto his horse. Where did he take her? What will happen to her?

When Sister and I hunt for wood to start a fire at dawn, Uncle asks if we've seen High Jumper. I look for what's left of our animals, thinking my friend is with them, but I do not see him.

His mother thinks he is filling her water gourd at the stream, but as we stamp our feet and try to get warm by the fire, he does not come. My neck shivers suddenly, and I am afraid.

"I think he ran away!" Partridge Girl reminds us of the others who have slipped off during the nights of this terrible march.

I remember how he hit his leg with the rope yesterday, he was so angry. "I think he went, too," I say, and remind Grandfather that High Jumper wanted to leave a long time ago.

"Then there is no use in calling," Grandfather says sadly. One tear traces a path down his weathered cheek, but no others follow. He straightens his shoulders and spits out that if he were younger, he would run away, too. He would rather take starvation on the hills with the piñon trees and the junipers than eat this sick food out in the open with no hogan for shelter, for comfort. This is not what the Holy People wanted for us.

Uncle reminds us of the old prophecy that we

Navajos are always supposed to stay within sight of our four sacred mountains and the three rivers. If we cross one river too many, evil luck will come to us.

Everyone shakes their heads, murmuring in agreement, and no one notices when I scramble back into our blanket tent and crouch, pressing my hand to my mouth.

Seven holes inside

All morning, we think about High Jumper, talk about him, wonder where he is and what he is eating. "His moccasins!" Slim Woman exclaims. "They were wearing out. What will happen to . . . ?"

Uncle comforts her, reminding her that their son has thirteen summers and is not a child. He will survive, Uncle says. At midday, the soldiers blow on their bugles to tell us to stop. All the wagons rumble to a halt, the mules shaking their long ears in the cold.

I tell Sah-nee that I feel as if we should be rubbing ashes on our cheeks to mark High Jumper's leaving. Before, I felt there were six holes inside me, one for each member of my family who is gone. Now there is a seventh; I will never get used to these empty spaces in my chest.

We hear a bolt of sound

Both Grandmother and I are keeping track of our people who die on the journey. There was a little boy so ragged, he couldn't survive the cold. He was left by the wayside. Two old women behind us sank into the snow, unable to go on. I can see Grandmother's fingers fanning out — more than five, including Dezbah. Many we don't know are so weakened by sickness, they cannot go on. Their crumpled bodies in the snow look small and huddled as children.

This day there is a woman big with child behind us — I do not know her name. Her husband and mother, I think, are supporting her as she struggles to keep up. With one hand pressed to her belly, she shakes her head. Aunt knows that the baby is coming and runs to ask the *Nakai* if we can stop until the woman gives birth. But when she returns, we know the answer is no.

Farther behind, the woman drops, until I cannot see her at all. Then a soldier comes galloping down the line, his red hair sticking out from his hat. It is Hot Face, and he disappears around a bend in the land. Only we hear a sudden bolt of sound.

Grandfather stops. "That isn't . . . they couldn't . . ."

Grandfather and Uncle use an evil word. Tears roll down Grandmother's cheeks as Partridge Girl plucks at her dress. "What happened, what is it?"

The rest of us know that the blue soldiers shot the woman, that it is easier to shoot than to help.

My knees wobble as I walk. I dare not stop now, I dare not slow down. They might shoot me if I do!

I try to tell a story

When we stop that night — we call it the Day of the First Evil Shooting — we move like elders with stiff arms and legs. Kaibah gathers firewood slowly and brings it back with dragging feet. Slim Woman cooks flaarhh on the hot stones, but her fingers fumble the bread, and it falls into the fire to be charred to cinders. Aunt is not rocking Starlight in her arms but just sits gazing dully into the fire. Sah-nee and her mother and grandfather are even quieter. No one talks. Silver Coat knows we are sad, sitting so close to us that his bottom is on our feet. Even that does not cheer me.

Kaibah touches my wrist gently. "Tell us a story, please, Sarah Nita. We need a story."

A story is the last thing I am thinking about. It is the

kind of thing that comes from that other girl who lived in a long-ago, faraway place with her mother and father. Those days are gone. I shake my head; my lips are too numb to even speak.

Then Grandfather lifts his head, eyes gleaming in the firelight. He tells us about the creation of our world, how the Holy People cupped the mountains in their hands, like a potter, her clay. How they set the four sacred mountains to be boundaries for the *Dinetah,* how the three rivers surrounded us. His voice rings out in the stillness. One day we will once again live in beauty, the way we were meant to.

Aunt sighs and begins to rock her baby as I sit by the fire, gnawing on my beef. If I had a turkey wing, like my mother had to fan our fire at home, I would fan that spark inside me until it blazed up. Today it is not blazing; it is a small red glow only kept alive by Grandfather's words.

The fearful crossing

There is a dark slash in the land ahead of us. Grandfather turns and calls back, "It is the Rio Grande. The last river around the *Dinetah.*"

People grumble in the line around us; they know no good can come to us after we cross the river. I peer ahead; it looks like high banks sloping down to the river. I only hope it will not be too deep!

It feels as if all of us are like a horse, bunching its hindquarters to leap over an *arroyo*. People cluster closer together; soldiers are shouting, wheeling their mounts, herding us to the bank. The first ones spill over the edge, slipping and sliding down to the river. All is confusion, noise, shouting. Animals bleat and try to run away, afraid to enter the water.

At the edge of the water Grandmother hesitates. "I am afraid, Husband, afraid."

He reassures us that it should not be too deep and tells us to follow him. Holding Grandmother's hand, he strides into the water, driving our sheep, and we follow. We have to; there is no other choice. Kaibah holds my left hand, and Sah-nee the other. Partridge Girl grips her mother's dress, with Uncle beside. He is holding on to my other aunt with Starlight strapped to her back. Sah-nee's mother and grandfather are close by, shivering as the water rushes over their feet.

The water makes me gasp; cold, piercing, like a sharp knife, it slices at my feet, my legs. Sah-nee cries out, gripping me tighter as our feet slip on the bottom. Kaibah yells as she trips and stumbles, but I pull her up. It is like being in a whirlwind of bad spirits — the noise of the animals, soldiers shouting, the river rushing.

When I look back, I cannot see Aunt or Starlight. Only the black water ripples where I last saw them. Uncle is thrashing at the water with his arms, looking, but he slips and falls in, too.

"Aunt! Aunt!" I scream. Grandfather is too far ahead to hear, and Uncle is trying to get his footing. I am afraid to leave Kaibah, with the water pushing against her waist. Suddenly, Kaibah opens her mouth and screams, "Cmmm herrr, Wyllyum!"

Off to our side, a mounted soldier wheels his horse and splashes back toward us. It is Mica Eyes! He grabs Kaibah's hand and pulls her up onto his mount. Dismounting, he hands the reins to me and dives where Kaibah points — again and again. His hat floats downstream, and the horse tugs at the reins. Again he plunges under the water, and on the third try, he brings Aunt up to the surface.

Quickly, he tears the wet blanket from her back and slaps the baby's cheeks. She howls — loud, rising howls — and Mica Eyes thumps Aunt on her chest. Bent over, she coughs and retches, and a long stream of water spurts out of her mouth.

Hauling her behind him, Mica Eyes whips a rope around Aunt's middle, tying it to his saddle. He grabs the reins from me and surges forward through the icy water. I am so numb, I can hardly move, but I must! Calling on Changing Woman to give me strength, I slip, almost fall, and then get my balance.

Forward, I push through the current, until the water slips down below my knees, and I know I'm near shore. When I reach it, people are kneeling on the ground, calling out to each other. Some are lost, drowned in the river.

Aunt is leaning against the horse, with Kaibah still mounted. Mica Eyes unrolls his pack and takes out a dry blanket. Stripping off Aunt's clothes, he wraps her in warm wool. Aunt looks stunned, unable to speak, and I hold Starlight in her wet cradle board. She must be dried, too, or she will get sick.

"Up, up!" the soldiers urge us over the bank. Once there, they stop and build fires so we can dry ourselves. No one seems able to speak except Kaibah. Slipping down from the horse, she takes Mica Eye's hand and squeezes it.

"Thnnnk uuuu," she says. I don't know what it means, but he does. He raises a finger to touch his hat and smiles when he realizes it is gone.

This is the second time that Mica Eyes has rescued us, and I am beginning to think Sister is right, that he has no dark winds inside of him. But I have to ask Kaibah a question. "What were those strange words you used — that brought Mica Eyes to us?"

"*Cmmm herrr* means to come to us and help. And *Wyllyum* is his name."

Wyllyum. It sounds like a wind. Or a swift and furry animal.

A *happiness comes*

We sit by the fires, drying ourselves. Sah-nee unwraps the wet cloth from Starlight and tucks a rug around her. Aunt is too tired and cold to nurse, but at least we are safe. For a moment, I look back at that river that almost took my aunt and her baby. Someone is still crossing; someone was left behind. It is a boy wrapped in a blanket, herding two goats ahead of him. Suddenly he slips and falls into the water; then he is up again, moving forward.

Gripping Kaibah's hand, I ask her to look behind, to tell me what she sees.

"It's High Jumper!" We race back to the riverbank and get there as he and the two goats climb up to the top. With a great shout, I leap forward and grasp his arms.

Smiling, he says, "*Yah-ta-hey,* Sarah Nita."

"You're back, you're all right!" I say over and over as we walk to our fire.

Grandmother hurries up, hugging him tightly to her chest; Grandfather grabs his other arm; his father and mother pat his back until he completely disappears in a group of shouting, hugging people.

Silver Coat stands, nose pointed, making sure that bad goat does not make a bolt for freedom. The good goat stands there, head hanging. Now, if the goats aren't too exhausted, Aunt will have milk again for Starlight. But we must wait for the food that comes with darkness before High Jumper can tell us his story.

High Jumper tells about his journey

Somehow Aunt managed to stumble on for the last march of the day. Exhausted, she sits by the fire, holding a wailing Starlight and crooning to her. Kaibah and I milk the goats; there is enough to fill a small bowl, and we take it back. Grandmother tilts the bowl so Starlight can drink. Though some spills on her, enough gets in, so Starlight quiets and finally sleeps.

Huddled next to our fire, we sit on rugs waiting to hear High Jumper's tale. After our portion of beef and flaarhh, he sits between his mother and father, pushing the hair back from his face.

He tells us that he couldn't let those people who smelled like dogs' dung take our goats; that he followed them over some small hills to a sheltered place where they made camp for the night. What noise they made! High Jumper says.

Kaibah wonders about the children who were stolen; were they all right? And my friend answers that the raiders did not treat the children cruelly, that they were fed. He wished he could have rescued the three boys and two girls, but all he could do was get our goats back.

When it was dark and their guards were talking together, High Jumper took our goats from the herd of stolen animals. He put his hands around their noses so they could not bleat and led them away from camp. He found that by sleeping between them at night, he could keep warm, and there were piñon nuts under the snow to eat, as well as goat's milk to drink.

Grandfather lifts some food to all four directions, thanking the Holy People that his grandson is back. High Jumper's mother sits close beside him, handing him pieces of cooked meat and smiling. For a short time, we are happy.

We head for the fort

Grandmother stops to make fry bread and mutton stew. She says she needs strength for the rest of the telling, that just remembering makes her tired. I am tired with her, for my pencil has been flying over the pages for days.

Grandmother says she will not tell everything that happened, because it would take too long and my book would have no more pages left. But she says that after all of their people crossed the last river, the blue soldiers took them north, past the white man's town called Albuquerque. *They had to go that way so they could find firewood to burn and water for people and animals. They went through gorges and over mountains until at last they crossed the River Pecos and marched south to Fort Sumner.*

Shimasani *throws a piece of mutton into the fire and says angrily, "It wasn't a fort, it was a prison!"*

The meat sizzles into a bright flame, and I think it is like the flame that is in my grandmother's heart.

We come to the fort

Soldiers ride up and down our long group, pushing us together, yelling commands. Mica Eyes trots past, touching a finger to his new hat, and Kaibah calls out a greeting, "Ehllo." I hate that she knows the white man's words!

Soon, the people at the head of the line call back that they can see the fort. "The fort . . . the fort . . . the fort . . ." passes back down the long, straggling line. As we hurry forward, ahead of us are some low, dusty-looking buildings in a circle of green trees. On either side, land stretches out flat as a rug, pricked with green.

They herd us into a large dirt area, taking our animals to a corral. But High Jumper will not let them take our goats, holding on to them and glaring at the soldiers. "No!" he shouts in their language. "No!"

"Siddown, siddown!" the *Nakai* shouts, running from group to group like a skinny herd dog, full of his own importance.

Kaibah and I whisper to each other, "Siddown,

siddown!" The words feel funny and strange, like stones in my mouth. I am shivering, waiting until I can get up to go look for my family.

But the soldiers go from group to group, writing things on small white squares in their hands. Grandfather cannot believe they are counting us, as if we are sheep they've just brought in from the land.

The soldiers do not look happy

Hot Face is one of the soldiers counting our people. His mouth turns downward, and his eyebrows bunch together. Even Mica Eyes looks worried as he talks to another soldier nearby. Grandmother wonders how many of our people are at this Place of Soldiers.

Nearby are shelters made by our people who are already here: lopsided tents, things made of cedar bark and old blankets, one with a fresh cowhide draped over some poles, and others that look dug into the ground, like burrows with brush roofs. Some women are sweeping the ground near their tents while children play in the dirt.

I stand up suddenly, looking for Shidezhi, for Swift Pony, among the children. Is that woman bending over a sagebrush broom my mother? No, she looks too thin, too frail. But Hot Face motions me down again, and I sit hurriedly, afraid of what he might do to me.

"This is the Beautiful Place by the River!" High Jumper hisses into my ear.

My skin prickles, as if an evil wind is blowing. How could it be worse here? It must be better, it *must* be, and as soon as these crazy ones are done counting, I will be off like a bird, looking for my family.

They cannot keep us apart

Just as the soldiers finish counting, a bugle sounds in the distance. People are returning from the fields near the fort. A big crowd hurries toward us, breaking into a run. People rush toward each other, laughing and crying, searching for their relatives.

Kaibah and I begin to run. "Mother, Father, where are you? Uncle, Aunt, Cousins?"

I see a woman who looks like my mother from behind; her dress is even the same faded brown. I run up to her, throwing my arms around her middle, but when she turns around, I see a hawk-nosed woman with wrinkled eyes!

"Father, Father!" calls Kaibah, holding out her arms

to the people running past. No one answers; we cannot see my father's tall, straight body and kind face. We cannot see Uncle's long legs, or the short, plump figure of my aunt. They go past and go past, and nowhere is a face that we know.

Grandmother touches my arm and tells us to come with her, that they will make shelters and a fire for tonight. Tomorrow we can look again. It is no wonder you could not find them, she says, there are so many people here!

Aunt is busy draping blankets over the wooden poles while Partridge Girl plays with Starlight and our dog curls in a heap nearby. Sah-nee stretches out a hand to me, asking what happened, but everything before me blurs and washes away like water rushing over dry earth. I sink onto the ground, head in my hands.

Mica Eyes says that all the Diné are captured

The bugle wakes me the next morning. Kaibah complains that she's heard that noise too many times! Did she think things would be different at the fort? Just as on the Long Walk, we gather outside our blanket shelters to cook the flaarhh for our morning food. Food is given out before sunset, and Grandmother makes sure we save some for the next day.

Briefly, Mica Eyes stops by our group and crouches down to Kaibah's height. "Hrre uuu?"

Kaibah smiles gently and answers, "Guud."

Grandfather is impressed and asks Sister to find out how many of our people are at the fort. Kaibah stands and points to all the people she can see, then holds her hands up, as if asking a question. Mica Eyes seems to understand and draws a circle in the dirt with squiggly lines on three sides — to show the rivers of the *Dinetah,* we think. Then, in one quick scoop, he gathers every bit of dust from the circle in his hands.

"He means all of us!" Grandfather's mouth thins. He cannot understand how that could be. Then the soldier pats Kaibah again and hurries to join another soldier.

Grandfather shakes his head and asks, Did the white man find all of our people hiding in the mountains? Did he capture the *Diné* of Navajo Mountain and Black Mesa and the deep, forever canyon near the place of the setting sun?

No one answers.

Our men are taken off to work

Soon the soldiers order our men to follow them. Shouting instructions in our language, the *Nakai* struts like a courting turkey. Grandfather and Sah-nee's grandfather do not have to go, as they are too old, but Uncle has to. High Jumper stands up, wondering what to do, and one soldier drives him forward. He is not even a man yet, but he will have to do a man's work.

Aunt, who gathers news here just as she did on the march, tells us that the men are going to dig ditches to water the crops that are already planted. The soldiers won't even give them time to recover from the journey!

Kaibah grips Grandfather's hand. "I'm glad you are staying with us," she whispers.

I wonder if my mother and father are even in this fort; what if they didn't survive the journey? Or what if they slipped away during the night the way some of our people did on the way here, going home to the mountains?

We hunt like hawks

That first day, Sister and I help Grandmother and Grandfather clean our small place in the fort. We are crowded like bees in a bee tree, with hardly any space between where people sleep, rest, cook, and clean. With a piece of broom weed, I sweep the dirt around our blanket tent. Grandmother points out to us where to relieve ourselves, off to the side away from people. I wonder if I will always live like this, pressed in among people this way, never having a space to be alone. We spread through the fort, taking up every piece of ground, many, many more of us than were on the march. And that doesn't even count the Mescalero Apaches — our old enemies — who are camped in a different part of the fort.

Together, Kaibah and I go from group to group, asking if anyone has seen my mother, Glenbah of the Salt People, or my father, Long Mustache of the Bitter Water People. "No, child," an old grandmother answers us, "but I will ask. Who are you?"

We tell her our names and clans, pointing to our tent. But no matter how many shelters we stop in front of, no matter how often we ask, I cannot see my mother, I can't see my father.

The men have bent shoulders

When the light slants low over the dusty ground, we hear the bugle far away. Soon the men appear, walking slowly with bent shoulders. High Jumper and Uncle walk up to us, breathing heavily. Uncle groans. "All day digging ditches out there. For what? I do not know. Others helped mix up clay to make adobe buildings. Not for us!" Uncle tries to spit but can't because he's so parched. Grandmother holds up a gourd filled with water she'd gotten from the river that day. It is not good water, but it is all we have. We must drink it.

Sinking down to the ground, Uncle drinks deeply and sighs again. "The Beautiful Place by the River!"

High Jumper's voice is hard and bitter as he says that the only true thing in that name is *river*. Beyond the fort, I can see it sparkling in the slanting light. I want to add that *beautiful* is true, also, but I keep my mouth shut.

Grandmother does not say *hush,* nor does Grandfather. We are becoming bitter, like some weed in the field full of salt and poison that sheep will not eat. And when the soldiers give out the meat that night, Grandfather distributes the pieces to people nearby. Uncle is too tired to do it, even though Grandmother has brewed him some sagebrush tea from her bag of herbs. It does not help utter weariness; it does not help heartbreak.

I am afraid to find out about my family

The next day the bugle wakes us, again; we chew on tough meat and cooked flaarhh — again. The men go off to work, with High Jumper, while we try to clean the tent site. Aunt is worried about finding enough cliffrose bark to put under Starlight's bottom, and wonders if we are allowed to leave the compound to find some. When the *Nakai* comes back from the fields, Aunt says she will ask.

Again, Sister and I go from shelter to shelter, peering into the darkness of the earth mounds, calling out our question. It is rude to enter a person's home without announcing yourself, so we always say that it is Sarah Nita of the Salt Clan and her sister, Kaibah, looking for their parents.

But the wrinkled, sad faces we see, the tired voices we hear, do not belong to us.

"What do you think happened to them?" my sister asks in a small voice.

I cannot answer and feel like Smallest One hiding in the bottom of the burrow, afraid to come out into the open.

We get clean again

The next morning I wake and see Sah-nee helping Grandmother outside our tent. With sticks, they are beating our blankets, making clouds of dust smoke up. Grandmother wishes she could wash everything — our rugs, blankets, us, even Silver Coat.

Sah-nee wishes she could take a bath, and Grandfather says we could use the river near the fort. But what if it makes the soldiers angry? Aunt wonders. Grandfather says we should just go wash ourselves; if we are not allowed to, someone will come to tell us.

Gathering up our blankets, we head for the river, but first we must pass a soldier keeping guard. Aunt points to our bundles and to the river, saying, *"Agua,"* the Mexican word. The soldier waves us on, though I do not like the way he looks at my two aunts; it reminds me of the way our men look at horses, thinking about how strong they are or how swift.

We hurry past the adobe buildings to the waterside, finding a place near some cottonwoods to bathe. Other women are kneeling by the river, rubbing their blankets and dresses with gravel, and filling their gourds.

"Don't take your dresses off," cautions one of the women. She tells us that some of the soldiers are cruel to our women, and Aunt nods. She knows what that means, but I do not.

While I hold Starlight, my aunts and Grandmother wade into the river, shivering at the cold. Even though it is the Time of Sudden Spring Storms, the water is not warm yet. Grabbing some gravel from the bottom, they scrub their bodies and dresses, dip in quickly, and let the water flow through their hair. Grandmother's long, gray hair streams out, and when she comes up, her eyes are sparkling.

"Clean!" she calls, wading onto the bank. She says she feels like a human being again.

Sah-nee, Partridge Girl, Kaibah, and I wade in, rubbing our skin with gravel, then scrubbing our dresses. Aunt and Grandmother keep watch over us from the bank, and I wonder what they would do if a soldier were cruel to us. Shivering and chattering, we hop up and down on the bank.

As we get dry in the warm sun, I watch Starlight try to grab the shafts of sunlight. It is almost a good day in this bad place.

I wonder if she is my mother

At the end of the day, after Uncle and High Jumper return, I look around the compound. Fires are flickering in the dusk; dogs are barking, goats and sheep are bleating. Now we must keep Silver Coat tied by a rope; Aunt says it is the rule here, and our goats are kept in a ditch Grandfather dug next to our shelter. He is taking no chances that they will be stolen again!

As I look around, I notice three women coming out of the adobe buildings where the soldiers live. Grandfather thinks they might be sweeping the soldiers' rooms or cooking their food. "Slaves!" adds Aunt. Jumping up from the ground, Kaibah and I race toward the women. Does one have my mother's shape?

The first woman we catch up to is short and squat, not like my mother at all. She looks weary, almost disgusted with herself as her moccasins scuff the dirt. The second woman who goes by is lean and thin as a juniper bush — not my mother. Quickly, I step up to the third woman, whose head is bowed.

"My mother?" I ask softly. "Glenbah?"

Her head snaps up as she turns toward me. "Mother?" I ask again, not sure who is before me. She is much thinner than my mother, though her face is a little like hers, but where once my own mother had a soft and gentle look, this woman's face is hard as flint.

"Sarah Nita?" she whispers. "My daughter?"

We grip each other tightly, crying and shouting, "My mother! My daughter! My mother! My daughter!" rocking back and forth.

Kaibah, who has held back, throws herself at Mother, wrapping her arms around her slight body. It looks as if that evil giant who devoured human beings had bitten chunks out of my mother, leaving a smaller, thinner woman.

"Oh, my daughters, my daughters!" she says over and over like a Blessingway chant that will heal us and make us well again.

Where is my father?

Grandfather leads us over to our fire and makes us sit on a rug. He tells my mother that Sister and I were so brave, journeying all the way to *tseyi,* and that we kept up all the way on the Long Walk.

Grandmother hands her a piece of warm bread while I speak one word: "Father?"

Mother says soon she will take us to him, but that he is not as he was. She does not know if he has some illness or if he is sick at heart. Grandmother shakes her head, saying that many of our people have died from disease and heartbreak.

But I want them to stop talking so I can ask more questions. What of my cousins, what of Uncle and Aunt? When I finally have a chance to ask, Mother smiles for the first time and says that they escaped from the first fort the soldiers took us to, going back to the mountains.

When Silver Coat darts forward and licks Mother's ankles and hands, she hugs him fiercely. Now we are all together again; the only person we need to complete our circle is Father. But I am afraid to say his name again.

We see our father

With Kaibah on one side and me on the other, Mother walks across the dusty compound. On the way, Kaibah practices her English words, the ones she's learned from Mica Eyes: *Siddown. Cmmm herr. Ehllo. Hrre uuu.* "Isn't that good, Sarah Nita?" I think she is hoping to impress my father when we find him, but I am too frightened to speak.

Suddenly, Mother ducks into a lopsided shelter, made from sheets of bark leaning together. Dirt is piled up around the outside, to keep the bark from blowing away. A ragged blanket is pulled back from the door.

"Husband?" she calls softly. "I have a wonderful surprise for you."

Silence from inside. Kaibah pulls on Mother's hand, wondering if Father is sick. Mother just motions us gently inside, gesturing toward a blanket on the ground.

Lying there is a shape that could be my father, but I cannot see his face or hear his voice. *Oh, don't let him sound like Half-Alive Man!* I pray.

"Father?" Kaibah steps forward, the bravest this time. Touching his knee, she tells him that his daughters are here, that we have survived the long march and have come all this way to be with him again.

With a groan, he holds out his arms and clasps her to his chest, rocking her back and forth. When he calls our names, when I can hear *my father* in his words, then I leap forward, clasping his shoulder and burying my face in it. Even then, I cannot speak but just touch him, feeling how his bones jut up under his skin.

I am afraid

Suddenly, great coughs rack his body, and he leans forward, gasping for air. Sister and I jump back while Mother runs forward with a bowl of water. Finally, after a terrible time when I thought he would die from coughing, he is able to sip a little water and settle back onto the blanket again. He is too tired to say good-bye; only his eyelashes flutter when Kaibah and I whisper, "Rest, my father."

Outside the shelter I hug Mother so close, she cries out. *If I hold them both tight enough, if I can get medicine, if I tell stories to chase away sorrow, then Father will not die.*

But I don't tell her that, I only ask if we should move our sheepskin rugs into their shelter. Her face brightens, the way it did when she saw a lucky yellow bird in a tree by our hogan. She says that there is room for all of us, and when she has to work for the soldiers, we can care for Father. Maybe the sight of his daughters will make him well again.

We leave Grandmother's shelter

Running through the camp, dodging children, goats, and dogs, Kaibah and I reach Grandmother's shelter, where they are still sitting around the fire outside, talking.

Words tumble out of my mouth, about Father, his terrible cough, how we are moving to their shelter, and does Grandmother have any herbs to help. With a gentle smile, Sah-nee gathers up our old sheepskins and hands them to Kaibah. "These have come a long way," my friend says.

Aunt heaps a clean blanket on top and some cooked bread. Grandmother rummages in her leather herb pouch, coming up with a handful of crushed gray leaves. She tells me to brew them in a pot of water until it boils, then let it cool off the fire. Father should sip it whenever he is thirsty.

Grandfather wishes he could find someone to do a Ghostway ceremony to heal Father and bring him back into *hozho,* harmony, with the world. But Uncle snaps that that will be impossible; they could not pay the *hatali,* the singer, and he would not have the things necessary for the healing way.

"If I were your father," Aunt says softly, cradling her

sleeping baby, "I would be healed once I had my two daughters again."

I hope you are right, my aunt, I pray you are right.

I dream of rescue

That night I think I will never sleep. Listening to my father's harsh breathing reminds me of living with Half-Alive Man, and I curl so close to my sister that she pokes me in the ribs to make me move away. Mother sleeps beside Father, a clay bowl filled with Grandmother's medicine nearby. When he coughs during the night, I hear him sipping the brew and sighing.

Through the partly opened door blanket I see moonlight on the ground outside. Some night creature scuttles through a shining path so fast, I can't see if it is a rat or something else. Silver Coat howls mournfully outside, and I go outside to hush him. Soldiers tramp back and forth around the edges of the compound, keeping watch. Their long, black shadows slip along the ground.

They are afraid we will run away; and wouldn't we? If we had enough food, if we had our horses back, wouldn't we be gone by morning if we could?

Finally, I go inside and sleep just before dawn. In a

dream, I have my old horse back and jump onto his back from a boulder, grabbing the rope nosepiece. Trotting gently, I make my way through all the broken shelters in this evil fort, coming to my parents' place. Holding out a hand, I help my father onto the horse, and Mother climbs in front. Somehow there is room for Kaibah, too, and with our dog loping beside us, we canter off, far away from the earth-colored buildings, far away from the blue soldiers, back to our red land, our hogans, our sheep, and our crops that grow in the hot sun.

I think about food for my father

The next day, I decide that we must start healing my father. The first thing is to make the shelter more weather-proof. The winds at night come right through the cracks between the bark pieces, and if rain ever falls, he will be soaked.

After Mother goes off to clean the soldiers' houses, and after asking permission from a soldier standing guard, Kaibah and I head away from the compound. We do not use words, only point toward some far trees. Then I hear steps running behind me, and crouch down, thinking it might be a soldier. But it is High Jumper! He tells me we cannot go outside the fort without him, that it is not safe; there are Comanches beyond the fort, and other dangers. He waves his hand, and I wonder if he means what that woman at the river warned us about — that some of the soldiers are cruel to our women.

To one side we see the fields; today is the white people's day of rest, and no one is working. We tramp and tramp through the new green grass, collecting armfuls to feed our goats. Other people are already ahead of us, pulling up grass to put under their babies' bottoms and looking for food and wood.

When we finally reach the trees, there is only one left with any bark on it. All the others have been stripped clean. High Jumper cuts through the bark with a sharp stone, and together we pull off a large piece. Then we trudge the long way home again, happy to have found anything at all.

When we reach the compound, we fix the bark over the holes in my mother's shelter, piling dirt over the bottom. Father whispers that everyone else is with the soldiers in the gathering place. There I see Grandmother, Grandfather, and all the rest seated, watching a thin white man in long black clothing.

"That's the Long-Dresses Man," High Jumper tells me. He says Aunt told him about them, that they are like our medicine men.

The white man in black says many long words over us, but there is no corn pollen, no sand paintings, or songs, just words going on and on while the birds fly overhead and the wind sings. He uses the word *Jesus* a lot. High Jumper says Aunt told him this white man is very powerful. Maybe I will ask this Jesus man to protect my father and make him well.

Afterward, we go back with Grandmother and Grandfather. He tells us that we should have nothing to do with the Long-Dresses Man or any other person the white people pray to. Our Holy People and our songs are meant for us, to heal and strengthen us and keep us walking in the way of beauty.

I *dream of corn*

That night Father sleeps a little more quietly. I hope that Grandmother's medicine is working! I dream of our cornfields back home, how we planted the seeds deep in the earth where it was moist; how we watched the first green shoots come out of the earth; how we prayed for rain to nurture the plants; and how we celebrated when the corn tasseled.

I wake up knowing that I must find corn for my father. He needs it to get well. He needs it to heal.

We find corn in a terrible place

Before the soldiers hand out our food that night, I tell Kaibah that we must search for corn and show it to Mica Eyes, that maybe he can help us get some food for Father to make him well. We walk between the shelters, asking if anyone has any corn kernels or has seen any. No one has corn, and everyone complains bitterly that they need it. Their stomachs hurt from the white man's food, and there is never enough to fill their bellies.

High Jumper joins us, asking what we are looking for. We tell him, and he heads toward the corral where the soldiers have penned our animals — all except our two goats. By the wooden fence, High Jumper points to some soldiers feeding the horses.

"Corn!" I hiss. "They are feeding the animals corn!"

But we could never steal it, High Jumper says; the soldiers would keep us from doing that. As we stand watching, one of the horses cocks his tail and leaves manure by the fence. Kaibah wonders why we are staying here; shouldn't we be going back for our beef and flaarhh? But I hush her with my hand; I have a terrible idea.

Once the soldiers move away to the farther side of the corral, I hurry forward and kneel by the manure. Poking through it with my finger, I find some undigested corn kernels.

"Sarah Nita!" my sister protests.

Wiping it on the grass, I hide it in the skirt of my dress. Then we hurry back, and I don't let myself think about where the corn came from.

The white men give us bits of bark

When Mother, Kaibah, and I gather by the wagons holding our beef and flaarhh, Mica Eyes is helping Hot Face with the food. They are handing out small, stiff blue shapes to us. They feel like the inside bark of the cedar. Grandfather chews on one edge and jokes that now there is not enough beef, so they are giving us bark instead!

Mica Eyes takes Kaibah's arm and says two strange

words to us that sound like *ray-shun crds*. He repeats the words and taps the blue shape.

Ray-shun. High Jumper says the word sounds like a dog being sick.

In a quiet moment, I go up to Mica Eyes, tugging on his sleeve and holding out the handful of corn kernels. I try to ask him if we can have some, that my father needs it, but he just shakes his head and says the word we all know by now: *"No. No."*

Grandmother and some other women are complaining about our food tonight, that the soldiers are giving us all the bad parts of the animals. Aunt holds up a hairy ear from a cow, saying, "They think we can eat *this?*"

Another woman holds up a hoof, another the guts of the animal. I don't think I can eat tonight, and when we return to my family's shelter, I hold out some corn kernels I've washed hastily. It is not enough to heal my father.

I get corn for Father

I don't wait for the sun to come; I don't wait for Mother to wake to cook us bread on the flat stones outside our shelter. Calling softly to Silver Coat, I hurry toward the corrals before dawn. Stars scatter across the dark sky, and I wonder how something so beautiful, that shone over our hogan, can shine down on these ugly shelters in this terrible place.

By the wooden fence, I crouch and look for piles of manure. The edge of the eastern sky begins to lighten, to turn a dull gray. I can see a little better and poke through some of the horses' dung from yesterday. A kernel here, five there, ten in another, and just as the red edge of the sun lifts above the land, I rub two handfuls of corn in the wet grass and tuck them in a fold of my dress.

A soldier is walking around the compound, his heels making dull thuds on the ground. When he sees me he stops and calls out a command. I duck, trying to run away, but he hurries after me, grabbing my arm. I will not let the corn spill! Silver Coat growls at him, but I cannot hold on to him. It is against the rules to have a dog untied, and I wonder if that's what the soldier will tell me.

Head hanging, I wait for the soldier to let me go. With one finger, he lifts up my chin and looks at me. It is a long look, the way those soldiers stared at my aunts by the river. My fingers dig into my legs.

Suddenly, I hear a cheery shout. Another man walks

up, shouldering a rifle. It is Mica Eyes! I would know his voice anywhere — that low, soft sound. The soldier lets go of my chin, turns, and follows Mica Eyes, away to another part of the compound.

I dart home and scuttle into my shelter like Smallest One, still clutching my corn. I am not sure what the soldier meant to do; all I know is, he was dangerous, and Mica Eyes saved me.

My father is grateful

When the others awake, I don't tell Kaibah or Mother where I got the corn; I just say that I found some and it needs washing. Kaibah hurries to the river and brings back a bowl of fresh water for washing the kernels. They are not dry enough to grind, so I throw them into Mother's pot and wait for the fire to be ready.

Sah-nee comes from Grandmother's tent, bringing a bowl of warm goat's milk for Father. "Grandmother thinks this will help him to get better."

I mix it in with the corn, cooked and cooled slightly, and bring it inside to Father, but he protests and says he will sit outside this day. Mother's face brightens, and she walks off with a lighter step to clean the soldiers' houses.

Now I know that the medicine and the corn are helping, for Father stands and limps out into the sunshine. He says he feels like a turtle getting warm in the sun. Sah-nee smiles at him and says that the *Diné* food will help him to get well. A sudden, sad look crosses her face, and I wonder if she is thinking of *her* father and brothers, hoping that they got home safely.

Now he has medicine, now he has the proper food, now he has his daughters back again. But I promised myself that I would tell him a story to help him get better. When Sah-nee says *Diné,* I begin to see pictures and hear words inside.

"Once," I begin, and Kaibah curls up beside me. "Once there was a corn plant named For the Sky, because more than anything it wanted to be the tallest, strongest plant in the cornfield. 'Oh, how I wish I could touch the blue sky,' it said to the corn around it. 'How tired I am of having my feet in the soil, of never being high enough.'

"It asked the woman who planted it to water its roots every day; it asked the sun to shine down with all its strength; it called to the wind to blow gently so that its stem would be tall and straight. And all happened as it wished: Its stem grew up past the piñon trees, up above the red mesa, up to the blue sky.

"But when it reached the sky the winds were too strong and cold; the sun burned its new leaves and the tender ears of corn growing on its sides. The woman who planted it could not give it enough water, for its roots went so deep and so far that they sucked up every drop of moisture in the land.

"The moon spoke to it one night. It said, 'You have become too tall, you have reached too far. You are a foolish corn plant. Pray that you will go back to the earth again; that is what you are good for.' So the corn plant looked down, missing the woman who used to touch its leaves and whisper of growing and harvest, missing the laughter of the children who played nearby, even missing the herd dog who barked at night.

"The corn prayed for a wind to come, for a drenching rain. And it did. The rain soaked the soil around its roots so that the roots began to pop out of the earth. The wind blew fiercely, bending the plant, toppling its stem until suddenly it crashed to the ground.

"*Now I am home again,* thought the corn as it lay

dying on the soil. *Now my seeds will grow new corn chil-dren; now my leaves will rot and feed them. I have touched the sky, and it was too much.*"

I pause and sip some water from Mother's gourd. Kaibah and Sah-nee are still beside me; others have gath-ered near and sigh when I am done. Father nods in the sun, then opens his eyes suddenly and looks straight at me. He tells me he could hear the voice of Mother's fa-ther in mine, that those words have strengthened him. He reminds me that we are from the earth, that the Holy People made us, and someday, once again, we will put down roots in our soil and grow strong and tall the way we were meant to be.

Uncle fools the Bilagáana

When the men return from working in the fields, Uncle smiles mysteriously at us, telling us that he has a surprise. Aunt tells me that he and some of his friends were searching in the trash dumps around the compound and came back, hiding something under their tunics.

Uncle disappears inside his shelter for a time, then reappears. Grandmother teases him, but he just smiles again and says we will have plenty of food tonight.

We line up together to get our ray-shun, for Father, Mother, Sister, and I always join Grandfather's family. I watch Uncle go up to hand over his ray-shun card for his portion of beef and flaarhh. Quickly, he hands the food to Slim Woman, then takes off his hat and pulls his hair over his face.

"We all look the same to the white man," he jokes, and gets in line again. Soon, he returns with a second portion of food!

As we sit around Grandmother's fire, cooking the beef and talking, I look at Starlight. She is not as plump as I would like, but between Aunt and the goat's milk, she seems to be getting enough to eat. At least she is not wailing anymore!

High Jumper eats standing, one foot tapping the ground. He still reminds me of a horse about to bolt, and I worry that he might try to run away. But for this moment, I am hopeful. Uncle fooled the *Bilagáana* with his fake ray-shun card and his hair over his face. Any people smart enough to do that can survive the Time of the Blue Soldiers. I know it inside, just the way Smallest One knew she had to leave the burrow to survive, just as Scootnugh knew she would fly free into the sky one day.

Now we are together, my mother and my father

beside me, and Kaibah in front. We are not broken, like a rug that has unraveled or been torn to pieces by violence and sorrow. I think that sitting on this earth in a circle with my people is like sitting on some great rug woven by the Holy People. When I close my eyes, I can see Cloud Ladders in the corners, the hair of Changing Woman in the middle, and something moving along the sides. I think it is my footsteps making hollows in the red earth, heading home.

The story is in the rug

I put down my pencil. My hand aches from writing, and the shadows are long near the hogan. Grandmother sips some water and listens to the wind rustling the dried leaves in the branches of our shade house.

Grandfather walks out to join us, crouching beside Grandmother, the way he used to, long ago. "Sarah Nita," he says, and both Grandmother and I look over at him.

"I mean Sarah Nita my granddaughter." He smiles and asks if I am finally done writing the story of the Long Walk. I tell him I am and ask again what did he think when he ran away after the stolen goats. He smiles and rubs his leg where it is stiff.

"High Jumper never did tell us about that time," Grandmother says, "but I think it was much harder than he ever said. His toes were injured in the cold, and they've never been the same." She pats his left foot.

"But what are a few toes when Starlight survived? She wouldn't have if I had not gone after those goats," Grandfather says.

I see the look they give each other; it is like a piece of strong yarn binding them together. And I know now that Grandmother's story binds them to me, as well.

I stretch out my bare feet on the red rug. Beneath me are the patterns Grandmother wove. In the corner are Cloud Ladders; in the middle is the black hair of Changing Woman; and along the sides are yellow birds and the footsteps of a child.

Epilogue

❖ ❖ ❖

Sarah Nita and her family were in Fort Sumner for four long years. Each year Uncle, High Jumper, and Father went with the rest of the men to plant corn, squash, and pumpkins, and each year the corn failed and food had to be imported to the fort. Starlight grew and began to walk, with Kaibah helping her. Shortly before the Navajos were set free, Sah-nee married a boy, Adin, whom she met in the fort.

On the way home, High Jumper and Sarah Nita came to an understanding. Once they found good, fertile land, they would marry and build their own hogan near her parents' hogan. Partridge Girl, Grandfather, Grandmother, the two aunts, and Starlight went back to the Canyon de Chelly.

But Sarah Nita made a promise that each year in the Month of the Parting of the Seasons (October) she would come to visit them in *tseyi*. Only Sah-nee disappeared from her life, going farther west with Adin and his family. Kaibah settled down near her sister and raised her own family when she was old enough to marry.

Silver Coat lived for many years with Sarah Nita and High Jumper, breeding with other herd dogs and always producing the swiftest, bravest, and most gentle pups.

Sarah Nita and High Jumper had four children, one of them being named Sah-nee after her friend. This Sah-nee had her own children and a daughter she called Sarah Nita, who was sent to the white man's school to be educated, as the Navajos had promised in their final treaty with the U.S. government.

*Life in America
in 1864*

Historical Note

❖ ❖ ❖

The history of the official treatment of the Navajo nation is like the history of the American government and other Native American tribes — hostility, a belief in their racial inferiority, mistrust, broken treaties, and ignorance about the complex culture and rich, spiritual beliefs that marked Navajo life.

For many years, Navajo peoples had raided the white settlers in New Mexico, and in turn, the white settlers had raided the Navajos and taken them to be slaves. By the late 1850s, soldiers were stationed at forts near the Navajo homeland. A Colonel Canby decided to wage all-out guerrilla warfare against the *Diné,* as the Navajos call themselves. Canby and his soldiers destroyed their homes, stole their sheep and horses, and burned their crops. It was a brutal and effective campaign, reducing the Navajo people to near-starvation.

By the winter of 1861, twenty-four chiefs came to Fort Fauntleroy, later called Fort Wingate, to negotiate a treaty. The Navajos agreed to stop raiding, to live west of the fort, and to recognize the authority of the U.S. government. In turn, Colonel Canby agreed to protect the Navajos from their enemies — the Ute Indians and the New Mexicans — and to give them some food and clothing.

But the Civil War took his attention away from the Navajos, and without soldiers to protect them, the Navajos didn't have enough food, had to return to raiding ranches, and were harassed by the New Mexicans. In the fall of 1862, General James Carleton was put in charge of Indian affairs in New Mexico. He was going to show Washington that the "wild" Navajos could be "tamed." Calling them little better than wolves, he declared they must all be rounded up and taken to Fort Sumner by the Pecos River in eastern New Mexico. He thought that by removing the Navajos from their homeland — the *Dinetah* — they could then be taught the white man's ways: to farm, to be peaceful and stop raiding, and to become Christians.

Colonel Christopher "Kit" Carson was a known hunter, trapper, scout, and Indian fighter who was put in charge of Carleton's plan to conquer the Navajo people. Carson continued the policy of guerrilla warfare — burning crops, taking prisoners, and capturing sheep and goats. During the summer and fall of 1863, his campaign was successful. In January 1864, he and his men even entered the Canyon de Chelly, *tseyi* — a place sacred to Navajos and a stronghold for them — marching through and capturing more Navajo prisoners. Without food, without animals, they could not live.

By the hundreds, by the thousands, they flocked into various army forts near their homeland, although there were at least 5,000 Navajos who never did surrender but hid in the mountains or lands farther west. In 1864 the 300- to 400-mile Long Walk began as soldiers marched thousands of Navajos through winter snows to Fort Sumner, also called the Bosque Redondo and *Hwéeldi,* by the Navajos. At the height of this campaign, there were about 8,500 Navajo prisoners at the fort, along with 400 Mescalero Apaches, their old enemies.

Different commanders took groups of men, women, and children on the terrible march of up to four hundred miles, across Navajo land and New Mexico in a harsh winter. Snowstorms did not stop the march. People died along the way — from exhaustion, cold, lack of proper clothing, from drowning as they crossed rivers. Some Navajos escaped and went back to the *Dinetah* to hide in the mountains. The Navajo people also suffered from the white man's food — bacon made them sick, coffee beans were boiled and eaten, flour and water were barely cooked and caused indigestion. But worse than that, the sick, the old, and women giving birth were sometimes shot along the way, for they could not keep up.

When the *Diné* finally reached Fort Sumner, conditions there were not much better. Food was still scarce, yet the Navajos were expected to dig irrigation ditches, build adobe huts, and plant crops. For four years, the Navajos planted corn, hoping they could harvest their favorite food. But frosts, drought, and army worms destroyed the crops. In the final year of their captivity, the Navajos refused to even plant corn. "The land does not like us," one man said.

After a period of greatly reduced rations, more food was brought into the fort. Every other day, 30,000 pounds of beef were given out along with 30,000 pounds of corn or flour. Texas longhorns had to be driven across barren country by soldiers, who also had to deal with hostile Indian tribes. Finally, it became too expensive to keep the Navajos in Fort Sumner. Nothing had been done to "civilize" them. No one was taught to read or write. They were simply prisoners of war living in terrible conditions, subject to the white man's diseases of small pox, diphtheria, and pneumonia.

After a delegation of Navajo chiefs went to Washington to plead with President Andrew Johnson to release them, General William Tecumseh Sherman (the author of the "scorched earth" campaign against the South in the Civil War) came to visit Fort Sumner in the late spring of 1868. He was appalled by the conditions there. Theodore Dodd, the Indian Agent, told the general that the Navajos had been model prisoners and should be let go.

Sherman thought of sending the *Diné* to Indian Territory in Oklahoma, but Barboncito, one of the Navajo leaders, said, "I hope to God you will not ask me to go to any other country except my own."

Finally, both sides reached an agreement in which the Navajos promised to stop raiding and to send their children to the white man's schools, and the government promised them they could return to their homelands (now greatly reduced in size). On June 18, 1868, the Navajos began the long walk home again.

It is said that the line of *Diné* heading west to their homeland stretched for ten miles. When they reached the *Dinetah,* Manuelito (a Navajo leader) saw one of their sacred mountains, Mount Taylor, and said, "We wondered if it was our mountain, and we felt like talking to the ground, we loved it so."

Soldiers at Fort Defiance gave some supplies and two sheep to every family, as well as needles and thread. However, it was too late to plant crops by the time the *Diné* returned; the food promised by the government did not appear; and the Navajos suffered terribly from hunger and cold that first winter. With the white man and the Navajos, it was always too little arriving too late.

But the *Diné* survived and eventually prospered; growing in numbers, herding their sheep, spinning and weaving beautiful blankets, planting crops, and living the way the Holy People had told them to live. Now they could truly chant,

> *"Before me beauty,*
> *behind me beauty,*
> *under me beauty,*
> *over me beauty,*
> *all around me beauty. . . ."*

Historically, the Navajo people inhabited the desert and mountain valleys of present-day Arizona and New Mexico, using natural resources for food and shelter. They lived in small one-room, windowless huts—hogans—made of rock, mud, and wood. Their staple diet consisted of corn, squash, and beans grown on the floodplains of the San Juan River, one of the few reliable water sources.

This interior of a summer hogan illustrates how wood is necessary to support its structure. Hogan doors always face east—the direction of the rising sun. Navajos use a special seating arrangement inside the hogan: Women sit on the north side, men sit on the south side, and the west side is reserved for guests.

183

This late nineteenth-century photograph shows Navajo girls carrying tusjehs—
*woven basket jugs—that provided them with fresh drinking water while they
walked in the arid desert.*

Since the fifteenth century, the majority of Navajo families have tended sheep. Without sheep, surviving in the harsh desert would have been impossible. The meat provides food, and the wool can be made into clothing, blankets, and serapes— *ponchos. In the spring, the sheep are sheared, and the wool is washed, carded, spun, and dyed for weaving.*

Traditionally, the Navajo acknowledge the earth as their mother. Because of this sacred belief, they honor Earth and treat her resources with respect and care. Today, the Navajo Nation, the largest Native American reservation in the United States, is 3.5 million acres and extends across Arizona, New Mexico, and Utah. Shown here are the Navajo on the Long Walk.

Canyon de Chelly, located near Chinle, New Mexico, is treasured by the Navajo people because it sits between the Four Sacred Mountains: Hesperus and Blanca Peak in Colorado, Mount Taylor in New Mexico, and the San Francisco Peaks in Arizona. Despite its tremendous elevation—at maximum heights canyon walls measure between 800 and 1,000 feet—the mountains conceal the canyon from miles away.

In the 1860s, many white Americans feared the Navajo because of their nomadic and raiding lifestyle. In 1864, Colonel Carson led the United States cavalry into Navajo territory, burning crops and hogans and killing livestock in an attempt to change the Navajo way of life and reduce the size of their land.

Navajo captives at Fort Sumner depended on food rations distributed by the soldiers who held them hostage. Barren desert lands surrounding the fort for 100 square miles made it almost impossible for the Navajo to find food independently.

187

This photograph shows women and children who were among approximately 8,000 Navajo imprisoned by the United States government at Fort Sumner. Navajo women and girls wore woven wool dresses.

Pictured here are members of the Navajo Delegation to Washington, D.C., in 1874. Chief Manuelito (seated center right) helped negotiate the Treaty of 1868, which allowed the Navajo people to return to their homeland.

In the Navajo origin myth, Spider Woman taught Navajo women how to weave on a loom. Looms could be set up almost anywhere, making them suited to the itinerant life of the Navajo. The basic structure of a loom included two fixed vertical posts—sometimes small trees growing close enough to each other—and several crosspieces held together by cord.

In *hozho* we may dwell.

In *hozho* we may dwell.

In *hozho* may our male kindred dwell.

In *hozho* may our female kindred dwell.

In *hozho* may it rain on our young men.

In *hozho* may it rain on our young women.

In *hozho* may it rain on our leaders.

In *hozho* may it rain on us.

In *hozho* may our corn grow.

In the trail of pollen may it rain.

In *hozho* all around us, may it rain.

In *hozho* we may walk.

The *hozho* is restored.

The *hozho* is restored.

The *hozho* is restored.

The *hozho* is restored.

This Navajo prayer, uttered at the close of traditional ceremonies, gives the reciter spiritual strength and inspiration. Hozho *can be translated as harmony, beauty, balance, peace, or holiness.*

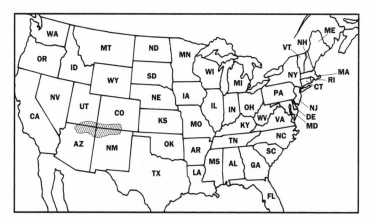

This modern map of the United States shows Navajo territories in Arizona, New Mexico, Colorado, and Utah before the Treaty of 1868, which reduced them to one-quarter this size.

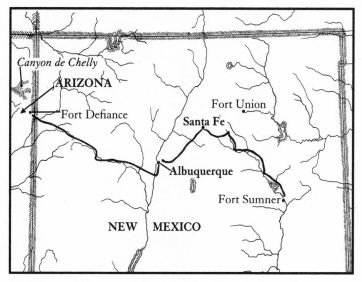

This detail of the 1864 Long Walk shows the approximate route from Arizona to New Mexico.

About the Author

❖ ❖ ❖

When asked what inspired her to write *The Girl Who Chased Away Sorrow,* Ann Turner says, "I am full of jumps and starts, just like Sarah Nita. I also used to push my nose into my mother's clothes to sniff up the safe smell of her. Like Sarah Nita, I thought speaking of terrifying things might make them come true.

"I cannot write a story without somehow seeing myself in the central character. So, although Sarah Nita is Navajo and was born in 1851, I see bits of myself in her.

"When I visited the Canyon de Chelly with my family, I stared up at the streaked pink walls and felt dizzy. It is a quiet place, a sacred place, and the air was cool and sweet with the sound of rushing water. Being there helped me to see that writing a 'diary' from a Navajo girl's point of view had to be different.

"There was no written Navajo language then; there would have been no paper and no pens to write down what happened. I knew that Navajos passed on their history and religion through stories — stories rich in pictures, action, and spirit. So I imagined that if I were a Navajo girl alive long ago, I would have remembered what happened in pictures. Dates would have no meaning, but the day the soldiers came would be fixed forever in my mind. The day my dog found me on the Long Walk would be a special time. Seasons, moons, winds, the time of planting, ripening seeds, and harvesting were and are all part of the Navajo world.

"The oral history of the Long Walk was passed down from the elders to the younger Navajos. The spoken history was filled with detail, action, and accurate memories of the past. In my book, Sarah Nita stores up all that has happened to her so that she can pass it on. When *her* granddaughter, also called Sarah Nita, goes to the white man's school and learns to write, then her grandmother's memories of the Long Walk can finally be written down.

"Historical fiction is a special love of mine, and I have written other books set in different times — some novels, some picture books. *Nettie's Trip South* tells of my great-grandmother's journey south in 1859 and the slave auction she witnessed — all true. *Katie's Trunk* tells of my ancestor who hid in a huge family trunk when the Revolutionary war soldiers came, for part of my family were Tories. *Grasshopper Summer* recounts the story of a family fleeing the bloody South after the Civil War, only to fight a battle with a new enemy in Dakota Territory.

"*The Girl Who Chased Away Sorrow* was a sad book to write, and one where I had to search for the positive, hopeful things in Sarah Nita's life. But they were there; in spite of oppression, disease, and a forcible removal from their land, Sarah Nita and her people survived and returned to their wild and rugged land given to them by the Holy People. I like to think of Silver Coat's pups playing outside the hogan that Sarah Nita and High Jumper built, and that they might look up at the stars sprinkling the sky and think, 'Now we are as many as those stars.'"

Ann Turner is the author of many acclaimed books for young readers including *Dakota Dugout,* an ALA Notable Book; *Through Moon and Stars and Night Skies,* a Reading Rainbow Feature Selection; *Mississippi Mud,* and *Finding Walter,* a *Smithsonian* Notable Book. She lives in Williamsburg, Massachusetts, with her family.

I warmly dedicate this story to Tracy Mack,
who first believed in it.

Acknowledgments
◆◆◆

I would like to give special thanks to Scott Smith, the Monument Manager of the Fort Sumner State Monument in New Mexico. He sent me a wealth of primary source materials about life at Fort Sumner (the Bosque Redondo) when the Navajos were interred there and courteously answered my many questions. His intelligence, breadth of knowledge, and generosity have helped make this project possible.

I also would like to thank Shonto Begay, Navajo artist and poet, who has given so generously of his time in reviewing this diary for errors. I value his opinion and thoughtfulness.

I want to thank my editor, Tracy Mack, who responded so enthusiastically to the first three pages of *The Girl Who Chased Away Sorrow,* and who has guided and sensitively prodded me throughout this project. I would also like to thank Zoe Moffitt for her meticulous photograph research.

Grateful acknowledgment is made for permission to reprint the following:

Cover portrait: Arizona Historical Society #28449, Tucson, Arizona

Cover background: Long Walk in Canyon de Chelly by Robert Draper, Navajo Nation Museum, Window Rock, Arizona (NTM 1970-1-3)

Page 183 (top): Photograph by John K. Hillers, Courtesy Museum of New Mexico, negative number 16038 (weaver)
(bottom): Interior of summer hogan #54619, Smithsonian Institution, Washington, D.C.
Page 184: Navajo girls carrying water #55621, ibid.
Page 185 (top): Indian maiden and her flock, photograph by William Marion Pennington, Azusa Publishing, Englewood, Colorado
(bottom): Long Walk in Canyon de Chelly by Robert Draper, Navajo Nation Museum, Window Rock, Arizona (NTM 1970-1-3)
Page 186: Photograph by John K. Hillers, Courtesy Museum of New Mexico, negative number 1129889 (Chelly)
Page 187 (top): Courtesy Museum of New Mexico, negative number 28534 (counting)
(bottom): Courtesy Museum of New Mexico, negative number 44520 (receiving rations)
Page 188: Courtesy Museum of New Mexico, negative number 38207 (women)

Page 189 (top): Navajo Delegation, Smithsonian Institution, Washington, D.C.

(bottom): Courtesy Museum of New Mexico, negative number 173524 (loom drawing)

Page 190: Navajo prayer, Museum of New Mexico State Monuments, Santa Fe, New Mexico

Page 191: Maps by Heather Saunders

Other books in the Dear America series

A Journey to the New World
The Diary of Remember Patience Whipple
by Kathryn Lasky

The Winter of Red Snow
The Revolutionary War Diary of Abigail Jane Stewart
by Kristiana Gregory

When Will This Cruel War Be Over?
The Civil War Diary of Emma Simpson
by Barry Denenberg

A Picture of Freedom
The Diary of Clotee, a Slave Girl
by Patricia C. McKissack

Across the Wide and Lonesome Prairie
The Oregon Trail Diary of Hattie Campbell
by Kristiana Gregory

So Far from Home
The Diary of Mary Driscoll, an Irish Mill Girl
by Barry Denenberg

I Thought My Soul Would Rise and Fly
The Diary of Patsy, a Freed Girl
by Joyce Hansen

West to a Land of Plenty
The Diary of Teresa Angelino Viscardi
by Jim Murphy

Dreams in the Golden Country
The Diary of Zipporah Feldman, a Jewish Immigrant Girl
by Kathryn Lasky

A Line in the Sand
The Alamo Diary of Lucinda Lawrence
by Sherry Garland

Standing in the Light
The Captive Diary of Catharine Carey Logan
by Mary Pope Osborne

Voyage on the Great Titanic
The Diary of Margaret Ann Brady
by Ellen Emerson White

My Heart Is on the Ground
The Diary of Nannie Little Rose, a Sioux Girl
by Ann Rinaldi

The Great Railroad Race
The Diary of Libby West
by Kristiana Gregory

A Light in the Storm
The Civil War Diary of Amelia Martin
by Karen Hesse

While the events described and some of the characters in this book
may be based on actual historical events and real people,
Sarah Nita is a fictional character, created by the author,
and her diary and its epilogue are works of fiction.

Library of Congress Cataloging-in-Publication Data
ISBN 0-590-97216-2
Turner, Ann Warren.
The girl who chased away sorrow: the diary of Sarah Nita, a Navajo girl /
by Ann Turner.
p. cm. — (Dear America)
1. Navajo girls — Social Conditions — Juvenile literature.
2. Navajo Indians — Relocation — Juvenile literature.
3. Navajo Indians — History — Juvenile literature.
I. Title. II. Series.
E99.N3T87 1999

813'.54 — dc21   98-48826

CIP AC

10 9 8 7 6 5 4 3 2 1   03 04 05 06 07

The display type was set in Elli.
The text type was set in Granjon.
Book design by Elizabeth B. Parisi
Photo research by Zoe Moffitt and Martha Davidson

Printed in the U.S.A.   23
First printing, September 1999

Reinforced Library Edition
ISBN 0-439-55539-6
November 2003